MW01702176

DEATH IN THE JINGLE JUNGLE

by

Lenny Levine

J K PUBLISHING

Death in the Jingle Jungle
Publisher: J K Publishing
Published: April 2024
Printed in the United States of America
ISBN: 979-8-218-38365-7

Chapter One

In the dream, I couldn't move my left hand. Helplessly, I stared at it, clenched claw-like around the neck of the guitar, my fingers grotesquely frozen into a chord out of Hell. My right hand, on the other hand, wouldn't stop moving. It swung back and forth across the strings, over and over, as the grinding, gnashing, eardrum-inverting sound blared out of the instrument like a thousand fingernails on a blackboard. I tried to sing but my voice was a death rattle, bleeding from my throat. From behind a desk that seemed to be four stories high, a hooded figure glared down at me. All I could see of his face were his eyes, two pinpoints of fire. Behind him, thunderheads growled in a malevolent sky.

"You insult me with this crap, Ernie," he rasped. "It's the worst piece of shit I ever heard."

"Please, give me a chance," I implored him, but only to myself, because my voice was still trying to break clear of the horror and produce the beautiful song I knew I'd written.

Suddenly, the sky turned a dazzling blue. Puffy white clouds with mouths sang in angelic voices, bathing my moaning in glory. The hooded figure became a beautiful woman, singing to me in a low, soothing voice:

Everything's gonna be all right
Every night's gonna be a good night
Don't you worry, just sleep tight
With Snorzium

My eyes popped open and stared at the clock radio. The commercial that had invaded my dream kept playing, the music growing softer while the announcer talked about gentle relaxation.

The sultry, dusky, female voice began to sing the jingle again, as the owner of that voice snuggled up to me and kissed me on the back of my neck.

"Mmm, they're starting to play that spot again," whispered Annie as she slipped her arm over my side.

I rolled over and held her.

Our cats, Pyewacket and Velveeta, marched up the bed on either side and started to purr, shoving their faces against the backs of our heads. They always slept a good bed's width apart because they hated each other.

"God, I was dreaming about Harold Gordell," I groaned. "This is going to be the worst day of my life."

The radio had turned to news now, and was saying something about President Carter speaking to the country tonight about inflation, as Annie snuggled against me.

"Then call it off," she said. "Tell Fred you've got the flu or something."

"I can't." I gave her a kiss and rolled over into a retreating cat, as I climbed out of bed. "I already wrote the jingle, and Fred's meeting me at Harold's office to present it to him."

"Even though he knows what happened between you and Harold yesterday?"

"Even though he sort of knows. I avoided the gory parts."

By now, we were both up, and she scampered ahead of me into the bathroom. I stood against the doorway and watched her. Even doing something as unattractively functional as brushing her teeth, she was breathtaking. She leaned over the sink, the ends of her long, honey brown hair lightly touching the edges of the basin, her beautiful breasts in profile.

We'd met nine years before that, in 1970. I was the bass player and lead singer for Generation Gap, a group that had been big for a brief time in the late '60s. We'd had a couple of antiwar FM hits, "Body Bag Rag" and "Good Tokes for Good Folks," and actually made it to Woodstock. Annie's success preceded mine, but was just as brief. Her group, The Love Notes, topped the charts for 12 straight weeks in '62 with a song called "Promises at the Prom."

They and a lot of other groups and artists had gotten screwed out of their royalties, and when I met Annie, The Love Notes were down to working in clubs. Didn't matter. I quit Generation Gap and became their bass player, going in less than a year from Woodstock to a backup bar band. Wasn't the greatest career move I ever made, but it was far and away the greatest life move. And so it remains.

"I still think you should call Fred, tell him everything, and cancel it," she said through the toothpaste.

"Then I may as well quit the business altogether."

She rinsed her mouth, even managing to look good doing that. "What's the worst Harold could do to you?"

I caught a glimpse of myself in the mirror, a bleary-eyed schmuck who couldn't keep his mouth shut. "Trash and compact my tune," I said, "then make sure I never work again."

She put her arms around me and we held each other.

We'd been in the "jingle business" for about three years. Just two months before, we'd finally felt secure enough to move out of our postage-stamp Brooklyn Heights apartment and into this beautiful garden apartment on 89th off Riverside, where we now stood clinging to each other, as the previous day's events torturously played themselves out in my head for the zillionth time.

***

I was in the semi-palatial, 43rd-floor office of Harold Gordell, music director for Picknitter and Ogrely. His desk wasn't quite four stories high, but it was impressive enough. I was sitting on the large leather sofa across the room from it, guitar in hand, flanked by another freelance songwriter, Bobby DiMango, and Stan Hook of Hooks Unlimited.

Hooks Unlimited is what's known as a jingle house, a music production company. They're usually small operations but they can make big money, since ad agencies invite them to compete for the lucrative rewards of putting music on a commercial.

In this case, Harold had invited Hooks Unlimited. Stan, in turn, had called on two freelance writers, Bobby DiMango and yours truly, to write one tune apiece. If either of ours got picked, Hooks Unlimited would win the account.

They'd supplied us with the lyrics, and we each had to write a melody. I'd spent the better part of the previous night agonizing over mine, and now I hoped I was about to blow Harold Gordell away with the memorability and charm of my music for Crummy-Cake. With an introductory guitar chord, I began:

One bite of Crummy-Cake and you'll see
We make it rich and buttery
'Cause it's made especially
Moist, moist, moist as can be
Crummy-Cake takes the cake for me

I concluded with a tasty guitar lick that took precisely four seconds, enough time for an announcer to say, "Crummy-Cake, the cake that's good to the last crumb," and waited through an eternity of silence for Gordell's reaction.

He gazed at me. "Hmm..." he said, triangulating his fingers and looking pensive. "Let me see the music while you do it again."

Dutifully, I rose, crossed the room, and gently placed the sheet of music in front of him, next to the picture he always had on his desk. It was taken at a golf course, and it was of him and Richard Nixon.

I retreated to the couch between Hook and DiMango and launched into the tune again, sans music and lyrics in front of me. It was okay because, by then, it had been burned into my brain.

I ended.

He glanced down at the music one last time and shook his head. "I don't know how you so-called rock 'n' roll composers think you're supposed to treat a lyric, but you've succeeded in totally missing the thrust of what we're saying."

"I have?" I asked.

"Yes," he said wearily, looking up at the gods. "You downplayed the most important line."

"Well..." I said, treading water and trying to figure out what he could possibly mean, "I thought 'moist, moist, moist' suggested a strong melody figure, so that's what I gave you. And of course the hook line 'Crummy-Cake takes the cake for me' had to be strong, and that's how I thought I made it, but I guess not."

"You guess correctly." Harold Gordell was a heavyset man with jowly cheeks and aggressively receding, dyed black hair that was pulled into an ear-to-ear comb-over. He had a perpetually dour manner. Even when he was kidding around with you and being friendly, there was a certain gravity to it. He wasn't being friendly at the moment.

"We intended to throw away 'moist, moist, moist' musically," he explained to his manicured nails. "The reason we made it repeat like that is so we wouldn't need music to emphasize it. You know, Dick Rodgers really knew how to put music to a lyric."

Dick Rodgers. Before he got into advertising in the 1950s, Gordell had been under the delusion that he could compose for Broadway. He never got any closer than Ninth Avenue. His biggest effort, a musical about Captain Kidd entitled *Oh You Kidd*, got shot down at the backers' audition.

"Nobody knows how to write great melodies anymore," he intoned. "Only beat, beat, beat. Rock 'n' roll is not music, Ernie. Maybe some stoned-out hippies in the sixties thought you were groovy, but it doesn't mean you can write it."

Stan Hook and Bobby DiMango squirmed on either side of me as I sat there, my mind recoiling from this ugly little moment. I had a fleeting memory of those days of idealism and purpose, when my music had been a part of something vitally important to millions of people. More recently, though, I'd written a jingle for Flake-Off Dandruff Shampoo that had lucked into a Clio Award. Which was why I now had the honor of being puked on by a guy with a picture of Richard Nixon on his desk.

"The entire thrust of the campaign," he finally revealed, "is that anyone can claim their cake is moist. We're the only ones who claim that it's moist AS CAN BE. Now, you've got the melody going down at that point, and it's entirely wrong."

"Then, how about this?" I said gamely. With a smile on my face and bile in my gorge, I sang the phrase with an ascending melody line. "We can even hold it out while the group repeats 'as can be' behind it." I tried to demonstrate the effect as best I could.

"That really makes the difference, Harold," Stan Hook earnestly put in. "We can bring it out in the arrangement."

"Or we can arrange for something else," said Gordell. "Bobby?"

DiMango was erasing something on his music, which I assumed was the melody going down on "as can be," and was caught by surprise. "Huh? Oh, sure, Harold."

He got up and walked over to the piano, writing on the music as he went. "I just realized I'd written a couple of the words wrong," he said sheepishly, as he settled onto the piano bench.

I don't remember how his tune went. I do remember it predictably wailed on the "as can be" part, but I was beyond caring. I was concentrating on how far I could drive my fingernails into my palms, as I wondered what the guys in my old band would've thought if they could see me.

DiMango finished, and Gordell gave it another of his weighty silences.

"Okay. Good, fine," he said at last, in simultaneous approval and dismissal. He looked over at Hook. "Stan, I'd like you to demo Bobby's version, just piano and voice. I'll play it for the Creative group, and we'll see where we go from there."

"Great. Great, Harold." Stan Hook lifted his lanky six-four frame out of the sofa in segments, nodding his head briskly as he reached for his coat. "We'll get it up to you later today."

I packed my guitar, gathered up my coat, and was perfectly prepared to slink out of there like all good business sense dictated, but Gordell had to go and put the icing on the Crummy-Cake.

"If you want my advice, Ernie," he said, as I was reaching the doorway, "instead of assaulting me with jungle music, you should spend more of your time listening to the great melodies."

Hook and DiMango were ahead of me. I turned and walked back.

"You mean great melodies like this?" I said, and sang at him:

Ooey ooey, they're so gooey
They're so scrumptious and so chewy
All my taste buds go kerblooey
When I'm eating Gloppers

I was singing the jingle Gordell wrote in 1957, when he was a lowly copywriter. According to the story, the client played the demo of the cretinous two-note tune for his three-year-old, and the kid had launched Gordell's career.

"Let me tell you something," I said, leaning closer to him, my voice rising in volume. "Cole Porter would've given his left testicle to write something as poignant and powerful as that. You're a musical genius, Harold. Maybe when you're dead, you'll finally get the posthumous recognition you deserve. I'd really like to see that."

Not waiting for his reaction, I wheeled and stalked out, shoving my way past Hook and DiMango, who were frozen in the doorway. I stormed through Gordell's outer office, past the open mouths and wide eyes of Hilda Kravitz, his secretary, and Melvin McIntyre, his assistant, and hit the hallway, where I stood panting.

It was somewhere around the third pant that I realized the full extent of the carnage I'd wreaked upon myself. I remembered that I was due to be right back in that office in less than 24 hours. I was meeting Fred Allenson of Allensongs there, to present, God help me, another jingle for Harold Gordell.

***

And now, that moment was near. Clutching my acoustic guitar in its leather bag in one hand, and the Fender bass I'd be needing later that day in the other, I slowly pushed open the heavy, polished oak door to Harold Gordell's reception area. It was the size of a modest hotel lobby, with not one but two Chesterfield couches, several wing chairs surrounding them like dutiful attendants, and, at the far end of the room, sitting at her desk, Hilda Kravitz.

Hilda was a pleasantly plump woman with blonde hair and big blue eyes. I figured if I got there early, maybe I could get a read on what the mood was. Hilda and I had always had a good rapport, at least as of yesterday afternoon. She looked up at my entrance.

"You?" she said.

"Hi, Hilda, how's it going?"

"What are you doing here? He's going to kill you."

I took off my coat and laid it across the back of one of the Chesterfields. "Is it really that bad?" I asked, approaching her like a supplicant to a queen.

She shuffled some papers around, avoiding my eyes. "If I were you, I'd leave before he gets here."

"What if I used all my charm and diplomatic skill?"

She stopped shuffling the papers. "I've never seen him so pissed. You were all he could talk about yesterday."

"Then, can I ask a favor? Can we not mention this in front of Fred? I didn't tell him the full extent of what went on."

That made her laugh. "Boy, you really are a masochist."

The door opened and in stepped Fred Allenson. Fred had airline-pilot looks: clear, hazel eyes that bespoke confidence; tanned, ruggedly handsome face; graying hair around the temples. He'd been the first music producer to hire Annie as a singer, and he'd given me my first shot at writing a jingle. Even though I'd won the competition for him, he said I would write twenty that didn't sell for every one that did. He turned out to be right.

"Wow, look what they did with this place," he said, looking around the room. "Hi, Hilda, good to see you again." She nodded demurely. “How’s it going, tiger?” he asked me. I tried not to smile in a sickly way, but I don’t think I succeeded.

Hilda glanced at her watch. “I guess Harold’s running late. He should be here any minute.”

“That’s fine, we’ve got plenty of time,” said Fred, settling onto a couch and opening his book of crossword puzzles. I sat down at the other end and became intent on fiddling with the fringes on my guitar bag. Several minutes dragged by.

Fred looked over at me with a knowing, satisfied smile. “Here’s one for you,” he said, reaching over to show me the cryptic crossword puzzle. “What’s a safe leap? Five letters.”

“I have no idea.”

“Vault,” he said. “A vault is a safe and ‘to vault’ is ‘to leap,’ see?”

I thought about it. “You’re always trying to get me into those, and they always make sense when you explain them. But I just can’t make my mind work that way.”

“You should learn to. As a lyricist you should be into all the different meanings of words.”

“I can’t understand this,” Hilda said. “Maybe he meant to leave me a note and he left it on his desk. He’s done that before.” She produced a key and went over to the door of Gordell’s office. “That’s funny; he left it unlocked,” she said, trying the door.

“Here,” said Fred, showing me another one. “Gateway to charm—entrance, or en*trance*. See what I mean?”

Hilda screamed.

We practically leaped, or vaulted, or anything else Roget would throw at you, across the room to where she was standing, staring wild-eyed into the office.

Gordell was sitting behind his desk, a half-eaten Chinese takeout dinner spilled across it, an expression of utter amazement on his face, a small, black hole in the middle of his forehead, and the music to my Crummy-Cake demo in his right hand.

Chapter Two

Detective Lloyd Raymond, a large Black man, reclined in the plush chair at the head of the conference table. He filled up most of it as he rested his clean-shaven head against the leather and looked at me slyly. "So, Mr. Lanier, did you and Harold Gordell get along well?"

"Most of the time," I said.

We were in a large room down the hall from Gordell's office. The cops had kept us in his reception area until Raymond had arrived, and now he was questioning us one by one. Hilda, Melvin McIntyre, and Fred had each been summoned to the conference room, questioned, and dismissed, and now it was my turn.

"Does 'most of the time' include yesterday?" Raymond asked.

"Well, not really. He was in a bad mood, and I took offense at something he said and told him so."

"Ah. But how did you tell him so? Communication is so often a matter of nuance." Raymond had a precise manner of speech and a deep, buttery voice, not quite Barry White, but about two notes this side of it. He shifted his position in the chair, pushing against the arm rests with arms that didn't seem to rest. They looked ready to burst through his suit.

"While pointing out to Mr. Gordell that he'd overstepped the bounds of your sensitivity, could you have brought up the concept of his death?"

Jesus. What did I say to him? My stomach shifted sideways as it came back to me.

"Oh, man, no. Not in that way. Hypothetically, maybe, but I didn't threaten to kill him. Is that what they said I did?"

"You see? Nuance." Raymond gave the table a light slap and grinned at me. "You interpreted my words to mean that some other people said something. Now why would you assume that?"

"Because they were hanging on every word of it. I gave the jingle business a story they could tell for years. But they didn't think I threatened to kill him, did they? This is crazy."

Raymond pushed the chair away from the table and stretched his legs. "Why was he holding your music in his hand?"

"I accidentally left it on his desk yesterday. Why it was in his hand I couldn't begin to imagine."

Raymond nodded his head slowly. "Mm hmm. What were you doing last night?"

"I was home, working on the jingle I was supposed to present to him this morning."

"Maybe you decided to go over there and present it to him last night. Can anyone verify that you were home?"

I thought for a moment and realized I could be in some trouble here. Annie had been out all evening on a session and didn't come home until midnight. I was alone the whole time, trying to write the jingle and contemplating my fate at the hands of Harold Gordell.

"Fred Allenson called me a couple of times," I remembered.

"At what couple of times?"

"I think between eight and nine."

"No one saw you or spoke to you after that?"

"No."

Raymond's eyes studied me for a moment. "Ernie Lanier, why is that name familiar to me?"

"Do you remember a band called Generation Gap?"

"Vaguely. Antiwar group, right? No, that's not it. You know, incidentally, when I was over in 'Nam, I didn't think very much of people like you."

Great, I thought, *a hawk from Homicide*. "Well, I can't speak for everyone, but all I was trying to do was to bring 'people like you' home."

He gave me a hard look. "Be that as it may, but in this case, it brings up something else. A picture was taken from Mr. Gordell's desk. Would you happen to know anything about it?"

"Only that Hilda noticed the Nixon picture was gone, and I noticed it too when she pointed it out."

Raymond nodded. "Now why did I know you'd say something like that?"

He lifted his linebacker's body out of the chair, loomed over the table, and gave me a tight, official smile. "All right, Mr. Lanier, you can go now. We're just getting started and we have a lot of people to interview, but I'm sure I'll want to talk to you again. Especially if I remember where I know you from."

Actually, I knew where he knew me from. But even though it had nothing remotely to do with this, I couldn't bring myself to tell him. The way things were going, it would only be another strand in the rope I could feel forming around my neck.

***

Never having mastered the technique of getting into a cab gracefully with a guitar and a Fender bass, I still managed to do it this time without smashing my nose against either of them. A glance at my watch told me, to my shock, that I was already twenty minutes late for the recording session at Magnum Opus Music. We started and stopped our way down Fifth Avenue for twelve jerking blocks, while I set a new personal record in knuckle cracking and tied a previous best in knuckle gnawing.

Throwing some money at the cab driver as we pulled up in front of the building, I unpiled myself from the taxi and ran inside. As I hustled out of the elevator, George Magnus, the head of the jingle house, was just coming out of his office.

"Where've you been?" he said peevishly. "We've already called a replacement."

My insides clenched. "Is he here yet?"

"No he's not, so it's your lucky day. We'll have to pay the guy, though, just for showing up." He shook his white maned head and frowned at me. "What happened to you?"

"I got hung up during a presentation at Picknitter," I euphemized.

"Picknitter?" said George, temporarily distracted from his anger. "Were you really up there yesterday, serenading Harold Gordell with his Gloppers jingle? It must have killed him!"

That's the advertising business. Get the message out.

"My tune wasn't what killed him," I said, starting to open the studio door. "Someone else managed to do that last night."

"What?" George's mouth fell open. "Are you telling me somebody *murdered* him? You're kidding, right?"

"No, I'm not, George; someone really did. Let me get to the session and I'll tell you afterwards."

"Sure, sure." He looked dazed. "I wanted to talk to you about a writing assignment, anyway. Someone killed Harold? Holy Jesus."

I opened the door and walked into the studio, surprised at the number of musicians I saw. Assembled about the room were not only the guitarist, drummer and piano player, but also five horn players and four string players. This was quite a production for a demo. I apologized for my lateness to the arranger at the podium in the center of the studio, who grunted and turned away. Slipping into my chair next to the bass amp, I began taking my instrument out of its leather bag, as a cacophony of warm-up scales, bleats, blats, and drum hits filled the air.

"Hey man," a familiar voice called out over the partition separating me from the guitarist, "why are you so late? You missed the preparatory phase."

This was the voice of Dave "Lick" Krulick, guitarist extraordinaire. At the age of twenty-six he'd already recorded half a dozen albums and was one of the busiest studio musicians in New York. The preparatory phase he was referring to was a little cocaine tête-a-tête in the men's room.

"You know I'm not about that, Lick," I said, plugging in and trying to hear my tuning fork over the din. Being a person of the '60s, my substance of choice was marijuana, although I'd certainly tried a lot of different drugs in my day. I never liked cocaine, though. It turned already aggressive people into prime assholes and made me feel more edgy than omnipotent.

"What's the matter with you? You used to be so hip," teased Krulick. "You were my idol, a charter member of the Woodstock Nation." I was only half paying attention to him, my eye glancing over the sheet music on the stand in front of me. "You should check this shit out," he went on. "I've got a new man, and he's put me on the Grade A list."

I loved Dave Krulick. There wasn't a mean bone in his body, so coke just seemed to make him happier. He was still talking to me when the engineer's voice filled our headphones, saying, "Okay, you want to try one?"

"Sure, as long as we're all here," said the arranger, looking pointedly at me. He counted it off. It was a 60-second spot for the new Arrogante sports sedan, and it was stirring and majestic, with strings soaring and horns roaring, in keeping with the grandeur of a luxury automobile. The bass part, fortunately, had no land mines in it so I was able to give a good performance on the first take. It was solid and self-assured and completely the opposite of how I felt.

We did three more takes, moved on to the "soft love song" version they wanted as an alternate, did the shorter versions, and wrapped it up in a little over an hour.

Krulick came around the partition while I was putting the bass away. "I'm gonna be appearing at Mikell's Thursday night, motherfucker. It's right in your neighborhood, so you got no excuse not to come. I wanna stare at your foxy wife while I'm playing."

"You moving to Cleveland?" I asked him, looking at his Indians baseball cap. His already thinning hair was getting thinner every day despite his age, so lately he'd been wearing baseball caps of various teams.

"Hey," he said, hefting his guitar bag and edging toward the exit, "you not only missed the preparatory phase, but because you were late, I'm late now. Mikell's. Thursday night, motherfucker. You owe me." He smiled and whipped out the door.

I found George Magnus in his spacious corner office.

"Come in, come in," he said and waved me over to a chair by his desk. "My God, what happened to Harold?"

"Somebody shot him in his office last night," I said, parking the instruments and sitting down.

"Incredible. When did you find this out?"

"This morning, shortly after his secretary began screaming."

"How did it look?"

"Beg your pardon?"

"His office. Did it look like there was a struggle? Were there any signs of violence?"

"Only on Harold," I said.

George shook his head. "Unbelievable. Do they have any idea who did it?"

"Not that I know." I didn't distinguish between what I knew and what I feared.

"A lot of people didn't like him, but to kill him, that's horrible!"

George was close to seventy years of age. He had a thick shock of white hair and wild, bushy eyebrows. I once told Dave Krulick he had less hair than George's eyebrows.

"Well, at least I'll only miss him in a personal sense," he sighed. "We hadn't had any business from him in years. But that aside, I wanted to talk to you about this chance we have at Burger Meister."

"Wow, fantastic!" I said, and meant it. Burger Meister, of course, was the number-one fast food chain in the country, and when they bought a jingle it might run for years. It would eventually be done in dozens of versions, with new ones being made constantly for special promotions. This was a plum de la plum.

"Now there are a lot of competing campaigns for it, as you can imagine," said George, "but there's only us and one other jingle house on this one. You ready to take a shot at it?"

"Like a shot," I said.

At that moment, a young, blond-haired man in a dark grey suit appeared in the doorway.

"Oops, excuse me George," he said. "I was just on my way over to KG&B and I wanted to tell you to expect a call later today from someone about doing a demo for CPR Breath Mints."

"That's great, Todd, do you have a minute? Why don't you come in?" The young guy stepped inside. "Ernie," said George, "I'd like you to meet Todd Winston, our new rep. Todd, Ernie Lanier."

"Pleased to meet you," he said, giving me a warm smile and looking directly into my eyes.

"Likewise," I said.

"Todd got us this chance at Burger Meister." George looked at him paternally. "Ernie is the fellow I told you about yesterday, Todd. I was just about to give him the lyrics."

"Hey, terrific!" said Winston, his smile broadening. "Write us a good one, Ernie; this could be huge if we get it. When it comes to advertising, these folks spend a ton of money."

"I know," I said. "They hold the pickles but not the lettuce."

He laughed, which was good. Most of the reps I'd met had a sense of humor slightly below the Three Stooges. They were a new, upcoming phenomenon in jingles. Increasingly, music houses were hiring young, bright eyed go-getters to stir up business at the agencies. In the '60s, I would've dismissed such people as suits. Not any longer.

"What are you doing at KG&B?" asked George.

"They've got a new creative director who's a good friend of a buddy of mine, so it should be a nice meeting." He gave me another quick smile. "And it was nice meeting you." With that, he was off.

"Lots of stuff happening," I said.

"Yes," said George, "in addition to getting us this shot at Burger Meister, Todd was the one who got us the Arrogante demo you just played on. And it's a demo-final, as you probably could tell by the horns and strings. If it's picked it goes straight on the air. Todd's really doing a great job." He stared dreamily for a moment at a vision in the space between us only he could see, probably eternal golf in Florida. Then he returned. "Let me describe this campaign to you. Here are the lyrics."

He slid them across the desk and I looked at them. They were actually pretty decent. Maybe this was one of the favored campaigns.

"I'm telling it to you in their words now," George said. "They want it disco but sort of folk music. It should be really hopeful-sounding but with grit and savvy. Something in the style of the Beach Boys, but not too much. They need four-and-a-half seconds somewhere in the middle for the announcer, and it's a 60-second spot that we should be able to cut to a 30 without having to rerecord it. Good luck. Do you think you can come up Thursday afternoon and show it to them?"

"I'll make sure I can," I said as I picked up my instruments in their leather bags and looped one onto each arm like a man donning a pair of water wings. "Hey, when that guy calls you about CPR Breath Mints? Tell him they're real Lifesavers."

"Try not to be a half-hour late," said George.

***

Annie and I emerged from the 50th Street subway station at Broadway and began bucking a brisk, chilly wind, as we walked east toward the Golden D'Or where we were meeting our friends Dawn and Gerard Mitchell for dinner. Not that I had much of an appetite.

"You should've seen this Detective Raymond," I said. "It was like I was auditioning for the role of chief suspect and could definitely expect a callback."

"I think you're being paranoid," said Annie.

"But not necessarily wrong. He said he knew my name from somewhere."

"Well, it was probably from Woodstock."

"It wasn't. In fact, I got the feeling from him that peace movements and bowel movements were all the same. He said it was from somewhere else."

Annie took my arm as we crossed Seventh Avenue. "So you told him, didn't you?"

"Actually, I didn't."

She gave me a brief, sideways look. "Well in that case, you're right to be paranoid."

A piece of newspaper that had been blowing along the street attached itself to my pants leg. As I kicked it off, I saw that it was an obituary page.

"I'll bet Dawn and Gerard are already into their second drink," I said, wanting to get off the subject. Dawn Mitchell was regarded as the top jingle singer in the business and Gerard, her husband, was a divorce attorney. "Just once, I'd like them to meet us at La Caridad." I was referring to a great Cuban-Chinese restaurant on Broadway and 78th that took no reservations or credit cards, had people lined up down the block every night, and whose most expensive dish was nine dollars.

Annie, of course, knew I was kidding. "Come on, stop worrying about how much we're spending. We don't have zillions like Dawn, but once a week we can afford to have dinner with them in a nice place. Besides, you're going to get Burger Meister."

"Please!" I implored her. I never expect to win competitions. People have greater hopes when they buy a lottery ticket than I do when I write a jingle. And to say I'll win one before I've even written it? I don't know what your image of God is, but mine is of a petty, vindictive Deity, who just can't wait to stick it to presumptuous putzes like me.

"I know, I shouldn't tease you," she said. "But at least we saved money by not taking a cab."

"That's like getting a free strawberry on your ten-dollar dessert," I said, opening the restaurant door.

"And at least your jingle career wasn't ruined by Harold Gordell, although this was a hell of a way for it to be saved."

"He may ruin it yet."

Dawn and Gerard were sitting at a table against the far wall. Gerard waved us over, then stood up and greeted Annie with a light peck on the cheek. He shook my hand. "How are you this fine evening, sir?" he asked with tongue-in-cheek formality.

"Fine and hungry," I lied, reciprocating his greeting to Annie by lightly kissing Dawn's cheek.

"Your beard always tickles," she said, her voice mellifluous even when she was merely speaking. When she was singing, if there were a mellifluosity meter it would be over the top. "I don't know how Annie can take it."

"You should've felt it in '68," I said. In 1979, I had what people would call a nicely trimmed beard. Back in the flower power days, a botanist would have classified it as shrubbery.

We sat down.

"Wasn't that fun, imitating the Andrews Sisters today?" Dawn asked Annie.

"Did you happen to catch the Knick game last night?" Gerard asked me.

"I was spared the agony by some other agony."

"Me too. I got stuck at the office until the wee hours."

"We were both better off," I said. "You know they've got to trade McAdoo and get some draft picks, don't you?"

"You're nuts."

"They've got to admit to the fans that next year we'll be paying higher ticket prices to see a rebuilding team."

The Knicks were his favorite subject. Gerard was an affable guy, about fifteen years older than Annie and me and a few years more than that over Dawn.

"I can't get over what happened to Harold," Dawn was saying as I pulled my attention away from Gerard. Her green eyes glistened as she clutched the napkin. "Everyone hated him but he was always nice to me."

"Someone must've hated him more than the rest," said Annie. "Someone in the business, maybe?"

"Oh, this is much too extreme for the business. It must be about something else. This couldn't be about the jingle business."

Gerard leaned in over the table and whispered, "Maybe Ernie killed him."

My blood pressure achieved lift-off. "Gerard!" said Dawn with a gasp.

He gave me a wink. "Let me know if you ever need a criminal lawyer and I'll get you one."

Dawn looked at me in exasperation. "This is the first time he's ever perked up when I've told him something about the business. And it's only a rumor, besides. You didn't really threaten to kill Harold, did you?"

"Not on his life," I said.

"There, you see? It's ridiculous. Nobody in the jingle business would do a thing like this."

"Seriously, why not, babe?" asked Gerard. "There's a lot of money being thrown around. You'd be surprised at what people do for a lot of money. That's why you have to be careful about it and protect it."

Dawn stared straight ahead for a moment, and then at her husband. "I couldn't agree more, *babe*," she said. And it didn't sound mellifluous at all.

The rest of dinner progressed normally with shop talk about whose voice was on what commercial and who wrote it, alternating with my little sidebars with Gerard about basketball. We made our choices from the dessert cart, which, if you added up the prices of its contents, was worth more than my first car. Gerard then excused himself to make a phone call.

The three of us sat for a moment and pondered our desserts.

"Gerard and I have been having problems," Dawn said, lifting a russet strand of hair from in front of her eyes. "I know I shouldn't talk to you guys about something like this, but I feel like you're my best friends. Gerard wants me to change our prenuptial agreement and I don't want to."

Gerard had met Dawn when she was seventeen, singing with a band at a bar mitzvah he was attending in Pittsburgh. Since he was a successful divorce attorney, he was familiar with the practice of the prenup long before the rest of us were. And since Dawn's net worth at the time was a couple of nice dresses, he had wanted to make sure that any possible future regrets would not be expensive ones.

Shortly after she came to New York and married him, she happened to play a tape of herself for one of Gerard's clients, a jingle producer. Even though it had been taped at somebody's wedding and the quality was terrible, the magic in her voice reached him. He suggested she learn to read music by taking sight-singing lessons and then give him a call, which she did. Now, ten years later, it was Dawn who commanded the lion's share of their joint income tax return. By plenty. Hence, the problems.

"I guess I still resent the fact that he didn't love me enough to marry me without a prenup. And I can't help feeling that if that's the kind of deal he wanted, that's the kind of deal he should live with. I don't know, I'm a mess. Do you think I'm doing the right thing?"

Gerard suddenly reappeared at the table. "Okay, got rid of that little business," he said, sliding into his chair. "Sorry for my absence. Wow, look at this!" He grabbed a spoon and plunged it into his chocolate mousse.

***

"I'll call her tomorrow morning," Annie said.

"They're in a tough situation," I said, as the cab she'd talked me into made its way uptown, "but if you ask me, she should give him a break and not rub his nose in it."

Annie frowned. "He rubbed her nose in it when he made her sign the prenup."

"So?" I shrugged. "Just because he rubbed her nose in it, that means she has to rub his? It's supposed to be a marriage, not a rubber match." I noticed that the cabdriver, during our inattentiveness, had taken us into Central Park. We were now creeping along the east drive, as the meter meted out its fiscal punishment. "At least you and I don't have their problems," I said. "We were broke when we met, and if we're ever broke again, we'll get there together." The meter clicked up another notch. "And in style."

"Either way, you're still going to worry about it," she told me.

I couldn't escape the feeling that, soon, I might be grateful to worry about something as trivial as money.

We got home several dollars later and were entering the building as our next-door neighbor Harris Hassler was coming down the hall. He was a thin, hawk-faced, elderly man, with sparse tufts of white hair and a no-nonsense gleam in his eye. We'd met him the first day we moved in, and he'd cast a disapproving gaze at my bass amp and Annie's electric piano, muttering something about this not being a night club. Now, he was casting an equally disapproving gaze at us.

"You shouldn't torture your cats," he said.

"What?" said Annie.

"You heard me, lady." He fastened the top button of his overcoat so emphatically, I thought it might pop out at us. "I almost called the A.S.P.C.A." He elbowed his way past us and out to the street.

"That man should declare his brain cells as a tax loss," I remarked, turning the key in the lock.

Both the cats were at the door as we came in, looking very untortured and glad to see us after having, no doubt, spent the last few hours avoiding each other. Velveeta had been my cat and Pyewacket had been Annie's when we first moved in together. It was hate at first sight, and nothing much had changed over the years. We sometimes thought they were the yin to our yang.

The nearest thing to torture that we inflicted on them was keeping them out of the living room. We'd never had a nice big living room with furniture from Bloomingdale's before, and they still hadn't gotten used to our suddenly protective attitude toward what, in the old apartment, had been a scratch-post theme park.

We hung up our coats, then led them past the closed cut-glass door, through which they could see the forbidden land, and into the kitchen. After we changed their food, we played with them a few minutes, and got ready to move into the bedroom for more serious playing, when the front door buzzer sounded.

The security in our little brownstone building was not top notch. There was no intercom. You just buzzed the person in, although tenants were encouraged to go out and see who it was. A wonderful system. I could imagine someone from the fourth floor coming downstairs, seeing his friend outside, then running back up to buzz him in. Conveniently, we were on the first floor, so I could just stick my head out and look down the hall toward the entrance.

A huge shape filled it, a shape I had unfortunately become acquainted with that morning.

"Oh shit," I said under my breath, as I went back into the apartment to hit the buzzer and warn Annie.

"I knew I'd remember who you are," sang out Detective Lloyd Raymond as he strolled down the hall toward our door.

Chapter Three

"Sorry for imposing on your evening," said Raymond, who didn't look sorry at all, "but I wonder if I could talk to you about a few things." He gazed at Annie standing next to me in the doorway and smiled. "You must be Annie Sands. My sister used to listen to your group 'til I wanted to tear out the record player." He gave a low, rolling laugh.

I invited him in, and Annie hung up his coat while I showed him into the living room.

"Nice place," he said, looking around and sitting down on our new sectional, filling up a section. Annie asked him if he wanted any coffee, but he declined.

We sat down in the chairs facing him across our new green marble coffee table and looked at him expectantly. Before he could speak, however, Pyewacket and Velveeta, stealthily approaching from opposite sides, pounced onto the sofa and into his lap.

To a cat person, this would be a magic moment. Raymond's reaction to it was to flip them off disdainfully with his forearms, rise to his feet, and furiously brush at his suit.

"God damn!" he muttered. "God damn!"

We both stood up as well. "Sorry," I said. "We usually don't let them in the living room."

"And this is the first time they've ever been in anyone's lap together," said Annie. "They can't stand each other."

"With good reason," said Raymond, continuing to brush at himself. "Even if I wasn't allergic to cats, I wouldn't like them. Didn't mean to scare everybody, but could you please ask them to leave?"

I was already in the process of doing just that. Finally, after I'd sealed them off in the bedroom and returned, Raymond sat back down on the couch, Annie and I took our seats, and he began.

"So it seems you were involved in The Death Tour."

This was the name the tabloids gave to an oldies tour the Love Notes did in late '74. We'd been rescued temporarily from the saloons we were working in by the oldies resurgence. Suddenly, thousands and thousands of people wanted to see the Love Notes again. We'd headlined a show called Sam Whitrack's Battle of the Groups, working, unfortunately, for the same man whose record company had screwed the Love Notes and every other group on the tour out of their royalties. Old passions and animosities were evidently revived, and before it was over, several people were dead.

Annie and I were the ones who finally figured out who was behind it, but I was the one who decided to wait before sharing these figurings with the police, a decision that had tragic results.

"I remember reading about the case," Raymond said, "and being interested 'cause I was into doo wop music at the time. Back in high school, me and my buddies used to do Coasters songs in the men's room, and I can still sing a pretty mean bass part. But aside from that, I'm wondering why you didn't tell me."

"I probably should have," I admitted, "but to tell the truth, I've spent the last few years trying to forget it."

"And in your forgetfulness," said Raymond, "you managed to once again withhold information from the authorities."

"Oh, please," said Annie. "None of that has anything to do with this."

He looked at her sternly. "That's for me to decide. And while you've been keeping secrets, Mr. Lanier, other people have been more forthcoming. A Mr. Hook and a Mr. DiMango have also told me about your ever-so-choice words to Mr. Gordell. And your phone calls from Mr. Allenson, as it happens, are not an alibi because it all took place after nine o'clock."

"The Chinese food delivery," I said.

"Excuse me?"

"He couldn't have been killed until after the food was delivered, and you guys found out it was delivered around nine o'clock, right?"

Raymond nodded slowly in mock appreciation of my acumen.

"Since you figured that out so nicely, maybe you can tell me why we found traces of cocaine on his desk."

This surprised me. "Harold was into cocaine?"

"Evidently. How about you? How would you feel about submitting to a drug test?"

"Just fine," I said. "I may have inhaled a little marijuana smoke in the last thirty days, but that's it. I'm not into coke; I haven't been in years. And knowing how obnoxious Harold Gordell was, I can see how he could've been. I didn't kill the man, Detective Raymond, I swear to you. All he did was turn down one of my tunes, and people do that every day before lunch."

"Harold had almost as many enemies in this business as there are people in it," Annie added.

"He only needed one," said Raymond, continuing to focus his laser-beam gaze at me. "And you're the one whose music he was holding."

"That's another thing," I said. "Why would I leave my own music in his hand?"

"Maybe you panicked. And then there's your alibi, which you don't happen to have, since no one called you after nine o'clock."

"Actually, someone did," I said, "or tried to. I got a job booking, but the answering service took it because I'd turned the phone off. I was writing the jingle."

Raymond shook his head. "That just makes it worse. If the answering service took the call, it could mean you weren't home. Who called you?"

"Some music house I never heard of, Face the Music. It's to play bass tomorrow night on a demo for Mussolini Chianti. I found out about it later when I called the service to see if there were any messages."

"A music house you never heard of? Are you in the habit of getting booked by places you never heard of?"

"My name gets around, and there are always new people starting jingle houses."

Raymond digested this. "You're not convincing me, Mr. Lanier. All I know is that you had an argument with the deceased, during which you raised the concept of his death; the music that was the cause of it was found in his hand; and a picture of him and Richard Nixon, about whom you admittedly have stronger feelings than most, was taken from his desk. And of course, you have no alibi.

"As far as I'm concerned, we've got motive and we've got opportunity. And if we find just one piece of physical evidence, however circumstantial, that points to you, you're gonna be writing jingles from a jail cell."

I swallowed hard, which, I'm sure, he took as another sign of my guilt.

He didn't acknowledge it, though. He looked over at Annie.

"I lied about wanting to tear out the record player. I used to watch the Love Notes on Dick Clark, and I thought you sang great. And even if you weren't hot like the Ronettes, you still looked mighty good."

He rose from the sofa and we rose as well. Annie got his coat out of the closet.

"You take care, now," Raymond said ominously as he stepped out the door.

***

"You were much hotter looking than the Ronettes. You made them look like the Singing Nuns."

I thought being flip might fool my stomach into undoing the clove hitch it had tied itself into. Nope.

We were heading toward the bedroom, where I'd stashed the cats.

"What's important," said Annie, "is whether things are so hot looking for us. And what we're going to do about it."

"Doesn't it feel like someone's setting me up? And it could be anyone. All sorts of people knew about my fight with Harold; even Gerard knew about it. And Hilda said it was all Gordell could talk about."

We had many friends and acquaintances in the business, some closer than others, but they were all new friends and acquaintances, people we'd only met in the last three years. What bitter blood might flow secretly through any of them? As one example, I didn't know the extent of Bobby DiMango's competitiveness toward me, but I did know he could recite the names of every commercial we'd ever gone up against each other for, and who won. He probably kept elaborate records.

And then there was Stan Hook, who gave new meaning to the term "agreeable disposition." He was so supportive, he was like your jock strap. A large part of his success in the business came from his genius at sucking up, so who knew how he really felt about Harold Gordell, or me, or anyone, for that matter?

"I guess all we can do for now," Annie sighed, "is keep our ears open."

I didn't have any better ideas.

We found the cats sitting on opposite sides of the bed, glaring at us.

"Sorry for the inconvenience, ladies," I told them. "Come on, we'll give you some supervised time in the living room."

They followed us out of the bedroom and through the apartment, getting interested in a big way as I opened the living room door. Letting out little meows that, to them, probably sounded like roars, they went right for the spot where Raymond had been sitting. They sprang onto the couch and, from opposite sides, of course, plunged their noses under the heavy cushion, trying to tunnel under it.

I went over to check it out. The way they were digging, they probably could have lifted the cushion themselves, but I helped them.

Underneath the cushion, coated with a sticky substance they immediately started licking because it was Cantonese lobster sauce, its glass cracked, probably from Raymond's weight, was the picture of Gordell and Nixon.

Chapter Four

Someone, obviously, had broken into our apartment and planted the picture, assuming the police would search the place and find it. We examined the door for signs of forced entry, but there weren't any. Nothing seemed to have been disturbed.

We came back into the living room. As I started to close the glass door, a tiny sliver of light caught my eye. It was glinting off one of the panes, about three feet up the door. I bent over and looked at it, and then at the lower panes.

"Check this out," I said to Annie, who bent down beside me.

"Cat scratches on the outside," she said, running her finger over the surface.

"See how high up they go? The cats must've have been climbing the glass."

"I'll bet it didn't sound too nice. And that must be what our neighborly Mr. Hassler heard." She looked down at them, sitting disinterestedly to either side. "We've got two eyewitnesses here, and they're useless."

As for the picture, our first instinct, of course, was to get rid of it. But then we thought it over.

"The killer's fingerprints could be on it," said Annie. "This could be evidence that exonerates you. I think we should turn it in to the police."

"But my fingerprints are on it too." I'd picked it up from the sofa, after pulling the cats off, before thinking about fingerprints. Once it was too late, naturally, we handled it with a handkerchief and slipped it into a Baggie.

"Doesn't matter," she said. "They know it's in your possession because you're bringing it in. Just explain to Raymond what happened. Make him see that if you were the killer, you wouldn't be waltzing into the police station with the evidence that would convict you. He'll listen; he seemed like a reasonable man."

"I don't know," I said. "He didn't think you were as hot as the Ronettes."

We decided to sleep on it, which I did in fits and starts, wishing things would start to fit. Finally, I realized I had no choice but to do it.

Annie said she'd come with me, but I told her she didn't have to. Not out of bravado, but because I didn't want her to cancel her job that morning. She was singing on a final for Pit Stop deodorant, and we might need the money for a lawyer.

I sat at the table, watching her eat breakfast as I picked at mine. With the Baggie-clad picture in a manila envelope, I zipped up my bass bag and hoped I'd actually get to show up at my three jobs today.

"I'll call you as soon as I know," I said as I stood at the door. "They supposedly let you make one phone call."

She came over and put her arms around my neck. "Don't think like that."

She gave me a slow, tender kiss that I hoped I wouldn't be remembering every night in some penitentiary.

***

The Midtown North precinct house sits on grim guard duty on the south side of 54th Street, just west of Eighth Avenue. A phalanx of patrol cars, marked and unmarked, parked diagonally side by side, stand at the ready with their back wheels poised against the curb like runners in their starting blocks. It's probably the only place in Manhattan where cars are allowed to park this way, adding even more to the sense of a greater authority at work.

As I crossed Eighth Avenue all my anxiety crystallized into one thought. I did not want Raymond to say my full name.

In every cop movie or TV show I ever saw, just before they read you your rights they say your full name. “Ernie Lanier, you are under arrest for the murder of Harold Gordell. You have the right to remain silent—” and the right to consider yourself fucked.

The sergeant at the front desk phoned Raymond to inform him of my presence and then directed me up the stairs to the second floor. I emerged from the stairwell into a cramped office area of four desks lined up in a row with a narrow aisle beside them, separating them from a holding cell. Raymond’s desk, as it happened, was about three feet from the cell door. Very convenient.

As he saw me, his face lit up into one of those big, crescent-moon smiles. “Well, well, well, if it isn’t Ernie Lanier!” (Okay, that one didn't count.) “To what do we owe this morning-after visit?” He rose from behind the desk and indicated a door I hadn’t noticed, next to the holding cell. “Come on, let’s go in here and talk.”

It was a tiny room with two chairs and a table. On the far wall was a mirror that was definitely one of those two-way models, and Raymond motioned for me to sit down in the chair facing it.

“Did something occur to you after I left?” he asked me.

I screwed up my courage and hoped I wouldn’t screw up anything else.

“Something occurred,” I said, “but not to me. Just after you left, we let your buddies the cats back in the living room, and it turns out it wasn’t you they were interested in.”

“Can’t tell you how unlovable that makes me feel, but go on.”

“They were mainly, in fact, maniacally, interested in what was underneath you, particularly the lobster sauce aspect of it.” I slid open the manila envelope and slowly extracted the Baggie with its incriminating contents.

“Oh, my,” said Raymond, as he watched it emerge. “Is that what I think it is?”

"It is the very thing," I said, starting to have trouble breathing. "I am delivering to you an item you could easily use to put me away. But I'm begging you, please, to think about it before you do. Someone stole this picture and then planted it in my apartment in order to, pardon the expression, frame me. They were hoping you would've searched our place and found it yourselves, but thank God you didn't. And now, instead of destroying it, I'm coming in here and giving it to you. You'll find my fingerprints on it because I handled it for a moment before I realized what I was doing. But you might find other prints on it. You're an intelligent man, Detective Raymond; you don't need me to tell you that. I had no reason to kill Harold Gordell, and I think you know it. But someone else did, and I want to find that son of a bitch even more than you do, because he's trying to ruin my life."

Raymond looked dead-on at me. No one had ever looked at me with such intensity. It was all I could do not to drop my gaze, but I knew if I did, it was over. I met his eyes and held on for all I was worth. Time seemed suspended. The room we were sitting in faded away and my entire universe consisted of those eyes. And as he mesmerized me with them, he spoke.

"Ernie Lanier..." *Oh, please, God, no,* I thought. *Don't let this happen.* "...you are one nervy individual to walk in here like this, but I think you're telling me the truth."

The walls seemed to materialize around me as the room returned with a whoosh. I let out my breath, not realizing I'd been holding it all this time.

"Oh, man, Detective Raymond, thank you! When this is over, Annie and I are going to take you to dinner at the Four Seasons. We'll even spring for the Five Seasons. We didn't sleep last night." I was starting to lose it.

"Okay, take it easy," he said. "I've been doing this a long time, and either you're the smoothest motherfucker I ever came across or you're an innocent man. My feeling is, you're an innocent man with problems. Somebody out there, most likely someone you know, has a serious hard-on for you. Now, were there any signs of forced entry to your apartment?"

"No. Annie and I examined the door and the front entrance to the building and everything looked normal. Of course, we're no experts."

"You don't have to be. Those toy locks you've got there are nothing to anyone who knows what he's doing. My teenage son could probably get inside your place in thirty seconds." He sighed. "You need better locks for a start."

"Don't worry, we'll start," I said, and then I remembered something. "Can I ask you a question?"

"Mmm hmm?"

"Were you guys watching our building yesterday?"

"Now, what makes you think that?"

"I'm guessing. But you knew we were going to be home before you happened to drop by last night, right?"

Raymond nodded and leaned across the table. "Yes, I did. Your building was under surveillance from six on, so the break-in had to be before that."

"Annie and I were home all afternoon. We left at about ten of six to go to dinner, so unless it was during those ten minutes, the only time he could've done it was when we were both out working. You know where I was in the morning, I was with you. Then I went to Magnum Opus. Annie had only one job, the Andrews Sisters thing."

"'Scuse me?"

"She was singing on a demo for Choco-lacto Milk Chocolate. They had to sound like the Andrews Sisters."

"What time was this?"

"Between twelve and two. That was the only time nobody was home. Whoever did this either knew that, or he was also watching the place."

"Well, you're the one who'd better start watching the place," Raymond advised. "And your ass. We're still talking to a lot of people, and maybe something will turn up on this picture, but in the meantime, it wouldn't be a bad idea to start thinking hard about some of the folks you know, and who might have it in for you. And get new locks."

***

I hit the street, found a phone, and made two calls. The first was to Annie, who said she never doubted for a moment that Raymond would see I was innocent.

"He sure had to look at me a long time before he did," I said. "Those eyes are going to be in my dreams."

As for new locks, they would, unfortunately, have to wait until tomorrow, since we both had a full day of jobs ahead. We figured that for one night, we'd just prop up a chair against the door. I was happy enough to be sleeping behind locks I had the keys to.

The second call was to Fred Allenson, whom I hadn't spoken to since the discovery of Harold's body. He told me Melvin McIntyre, or in his words, "that asshole Melvin McIntyre," was taking over Harold's job, and that our ill-fated presentation was now re-scheduled for Friday morning. He also told me they'd changed the lyrics.

"Since they had all this extra time to think about it, they decided to improve them for the worse. Do you suppose you could drop by my office around noon tomorrow? I think a couple of minor musical adjustments should do it, but let's confer."

"You got it, Fred," I said, hanging up with one hand and hailing a cab with the other.

***

Sound Judgment Studios was in the West 20's. Its owner, Mersh Hamish, had operated it for years doing Yiddish and Israeli records. His studio was also used occasionally for local jingles by the man I was working for today, Izzy Shleppman.

I worked for Izzy about twice a year. He was a short, squat, Jewish version of Stan Hook, who was tall, skinny, and Protestant. They both had the same anxiety to please. The major difference between them was the quality of the clients who enjoyed all that attention. Stan was someone who'd actually won Burger Meister. Izzy was someone who took used car dealers to lunch.

As I opened the studio door, I heard a familiar voice. "Steely Dan, now they were some interesting dudes to work with," Dave Krulick was saying to the engineer who was positioning his amp. The engineer looked like he was about sixteen, with a yarmulke atop hair that hung below his shoulders. Krulick noticed me coming over.

"Hey, all right! Now this gig is starting to get interesting. My man Ernie and I are gonna play some kickass shit for, what is it Izzy?"

Shleppman was sitting at the piano. He was actually a very good pianist who could play serious ragtime and stride piano. His jingles never sounded remotely like that.

"It's Bergenshnerfer's Plumbing Supplies," he said almost ashamedly. "What are you gonna do? They're buying a whole bunch of radio time during the Mets games this year. So, probably, nobody's gonna listen to it because nobody listens to the Mets, but I don't care, and the guy is easy to work for."

"Hey, man," said Krulick to me, "why didn't you tell me about Harold Gordell yesterday? Shit, that was unbelievable. Somebody really offed him?"

"Somebody off-offed him," I said.

"Like one of his shows," said Shleppman. "I used to play piano for him. He was always trying to mount some musical revue or other. That is, when he wasn't trying to mount the actresses. He was quite a go-getter, that Harold. I haven't seen him in years, and now I never will. Go know." He shrugged his shoulders. "So, you wanna hear this?"

Krulick and I both nodded, and the drummer in his booth rapped the snare a couple of times in assent. We looked down at our music, Shleppman turned to face the keys, and sang to us:

We're Bergenshnerfer's Plumbing Supplies
The place where pipe dreams really do come true
We're Bergenshnerfer's Plumbing Supplies
We back you up when things back up on you
We're Bergenshnerfer's, we are the best
Bergenshnerfer's, flushed with success
Bergenshnerfer's Plumbing Supplies

The music was the kind you might hear at a coronation, "Pomp and Circumstance" with the melody line inverted. "Sounds great, Izzy," Krulick and I said simultaneously.

After the session, as we were packing up and the singers were coming in, Krulick came over and whispered in my ear. "I'm telling you man, you ought to reconsider about the preparatory phase. I know you usually don't have eyes for it, but this is different."

"Come on," I said, "are you getting lonely in the bathroom? It used to be only women who went off to the john to powder their noses."

"Just trying to get you ready for the eighties." He looked at his watch. "Oh man, shit! Why does this place have to be so far downtown? Where are you going next?"

"Phil and Judy's studio."

"Come on man, put that thing in the bag and move your ass. We can split a cab and you can tell me about Harold. Did you really discover the body? That is so fucking cool."

***

Phil and Judy Sellers had a combination jingle house and studio on West 53rd Street, called Best Sellers, Inc. She was the former Judy Doherty, a singer who at one time was as busy as Dawn Mitchell. Phil's jingle house was even busier than that when they'd gotten married about four years ago. But by doing so, they'd violated one of the major unspoken rules in the business: Freelancers associate themselves with individual jingle houses at their peril.

All singers are freelancers, working for many jingle houses, and sometimes, singing on competing campaigns. Since they're only on the sound track, they're anonymous. You would never see, for example, an on-camera actor in a Ford commercial and a Buick commercial because you'd say, "Hey that's the guy from the Ford commercial." But the same people could sing in a group for both cars and no one would know. Consequently, jingle producers, not having to worry about their singers' conflicts of interest, tend to hire the same ones again and again, and why not? If you know certain people are going to do a good job for you and sound terrific, why not use them?

But if you're a singer who becomes personally, or romantically, involved with someone associated with a jingle house, other houses are reluctant to hire you. It's like you've become a spy from their competition. Everyone is still friends, but that's how it is. Annie and I were both freelance, but if I ever decided to form my own jingle house, and God knows why I would do that, her career as a singer in the business would be severely compromised.

I arrived at Phil and Judy's to find them sitting in the control room with Mike, their engineer.

"Hey, pard," Phil greeted me. "Come on in and tell us what happened to Harold."

Phil was a large, affable bear of a man with a dark cloud of blow-dry hair and a ruddy complexion. He got up and shook my hand, clapped me on the back, and bade me sit down.

"Hey, Phil; hey, Judy," I said, pulling up a chair next to her. She smiled at me as she smiled at everyone, with a look of nervous uncertainty in her eyes. It was almost as if smiling made her feel guilty.

"There's nothing much to tell. Somebody shot him in his office on Monday night."

Judy lifted her tiny, stockinged feet and gracefully tucked them underneath her, curling her body snugly into the contours of the plush chair. "I know a lot of people who would've liked to kill him, but I never thought anyone actually would."

There was an opening if I ever heard one.

"You think it was someone in jingles?" I asked her.

She looked over at Phil, who shrugged.

"Who can tell? This can be a rough business. Maybe Harold got rough with the wrong person."

"Like who?"

"Excuse me, Phil," Mike interrupted, spooling a large reel of tape onto the machine, "I've got the studio set up to start any time you want."

"Then why don't we?" Phil reached behind his chair and pulled a hard-shell guitar case around, sliding it toward me. "We've got the house guitar right here. I hope you didn't change any of their precious lyrics. They're chiseled in stone."

"I wouldn't chisel them out of a word," I said, trying to stifle the frustration I felt. It was tricky, working this private-eye stuff into normal conversation.

I gave the guitar a quick tuning job, got out my music, and in a clear Irish tenor, sang:

Derry Air's your airline
Let us take you there
Fly with us to Ireland
On your Derry Air

I hummed the tune with a slight variation, just to keep it interesting, for twelve-and-a-half seconds, over which some announcer would extol the friendliness of the old sod. Then I raised it up a tone and sang it again, the final notes ascending confidently, reaching cruising altitude at exactly 60 seconds.

"Great," said Phil. "We can really build it up there at the end. You and Judy can be a whole choir." And he wasn't kidding.

Mike ran off some copies of the music and Phil and I went out into the studio to rehearse it. We would eventually record a couple of guitar and piano tracks, and then I would switch to bass and Phil would play drums. In this way, the two of us would play all the parts of the instrumental track.

"Listen," he said as he spread out the music on the piano, "I really appreciate your spending so much time over here doing all this. It's bad enough that jingle writers don't get any money unless it sells. You're also doing for nothing what I'd have to pay three musicians and five singers to do."

"I just want to win this account," I told him. I also wanted to pick up the thread. "What did you mean before, when you said Harold might've gotten rough with the wrong person?"

A look of mild disgust crossed his face. "Harold had his own way of operating. I have no idea what he's done lately because I haven't been associated with him lately." He gave a humorless laugh. "There are a lot of people I haven't been associated with lately. I don't know what you've been experiencing, but business has been really shitty."

"I guess it's been better," I said, noticing he'd changed the subject and wondering what I could do about it. When it comes to this kind of stuff, cops have it a lot easier than jingle writers.

"Maybe I should start using reps, like Magnum Opus," Phil mused. "Agency people are getting younger and you've got to present them with a young image." He started to play the first few chord changes of my tune. "Meanwhile, let's see if we can win this fucker."

About an hour later, after we'd finished the instrumental track, Phil went into the control room and Judy came out to do the vocals with me.

"Say hi to Annie for me," she said, smiling in her tentative way. "The worst thing about business being so slow is that you don't get to see your friends."

Mike was adjusting the microphone, trying to find a good neutral position. I'm a little over six feet and Judy's a little under five. Finally he muttered, "I'd better use two mikes," and started to drag another one across the studio.

Judy looked up at me. "I heard you sang Harold his Gloppers jingle."

"It's really something how fast that story got around," I said. "Where did you hear it?"

"From Bobby DiMango. He was up here yesterday, dropping off his latest demo reel."

"Yeah, he was there. We were with Stan Hook."

She frowned. "Stan Hook always creeped me out. That 'at your service' personality of his, like some kind of robot. Boy, you know, he had a good reason to hate Harold."

Look at that; didn't even have to try.

"What do you mean?" I asked.

"Okay, you wanna hear the instrumental track?" Mike's voice floated over the intercom.

"Sure," said Judy. It began playing in the headphones as I clutched mine to my ears.

Forty endless minutes crept by as it took an act of will for me to concentrate on the music. We sang the melody in unison for three tracks and added three more tracks of harmony as, several times, I almost screwed up my own tune. At last, Mike said he was running out of tracks and we'd have to take a break while he combined the ones we'd done.

"What do you mean?" I said.

"About what?" asked Judy.

"About Stan Hook having a good reason to hate Harold."

"Oh that. A few years ago, Stan was trying to get his sister Felice, into the business. She was a pretty good singer, nice voice, good musician, but she was nervous in the studio. He used her in a group on a session for Harold once, and maybe Harold didn't like Stan getting his sister on the contract. Who knows? Anyway, he made the session miserable for her, having her sing her part alone, criticizing her pitch, telling her to sing softer, the works."

I believed it. Gordell could really put that sob into your voice.

"Well, it turned out Felice was very fragile. She'd had a couple of nervous breakdowns in her life, and this time she had the big one. They found her dead that night with a month's worth of her Valium prescription inside her."

"Wow, I never knew! It's amazing Stan could still work with Harold after that."

Judy smiled and this time, so did her eyes.

"Oh, no it isn't. Remember, this is a world-class ass kisser we're talking about." She called into the booth, "Hey, Mike, let's do these last three tracks already, so the Mormon Tabernacle Choir can go home."

***

It had turned dark by the time I left Best Sellers and headed west on 53rd. I had some chicken with rice and black beans at a place on Tenth Avenue and then checked my datebook for the address of Face the Music. It was 624 West 52nd, which put it between Eleventh and what used to be the West Side Highway. Since I was only carrying one instrument and still had time, I decided to walk it.

The block was made up of warehouses and garages on one side and a fenced-in park on the other. It didn't surprise me that I was going to a warehouse. Lately, new jingle houses had been renting them and turning them into studios. It was hard to make out addresses, though, as I looked at doorways that seemed to be blank. As I was getting to one somewhere in the middle of the block I suddenly felt myself being helped to get there. A hand clamped itself around my neck, something hard jabbed into the small of my back and I was hustled forward into the recess of the building and slammed against the wall.

"Hey, it's in my back pocket, man; you can have it," I started to say, but I was saying it with my face being squashed against brick.

I felt the tip of the gun being transferred from the small of my back to behind my right ear as the hand let go of my neck. It reached into my back pocket and extracted the wallet, then returned to my neck.

Okay, I thought, starting to sweat, now he goes away like a good professional mugger or he kills me. His already powerful grip tightened, mashing my face even harder against the wall. I felt the gun being withdrawn, as he moved back, now holding me at arm's length, and suddenly I couldn't stand it anymore.

I jerked my head violently to the side, scraping my cheek and desperately trying to look behind me to see what he was about to do. What I saw was a gun butt coming down, a fraction of a second before everything went whang!

It continued to go whang! in waves, accompanied by blazing, pulsating suns that filled my vision. And pain. Lots of pain. I sank to my knees and felt the bass bag sliding off my arm. Something heavy was being put into my coat pocket. I heard the sound of footsteps moving away from me. Whang! Whang!

It was after about twenty whangs! that I felt a hand on my arm.

"Hey pal, are you okay?"

I looked up through the suns that were now subsiding, into the face of a uniformed cop.

"I got mugged," I said. "Where's my bass?"

"There doesn't seem to be anything here. What'd he get, your wallet?"

I could only hear him intermittently through the whangs!

"And my bass. Shit, I've had that bass all my life." My head was killing me and I'll be damned if I know why the bass was so important at that moment.

"Do you think you can get up?" he asked and started to help me to my feet. I made it as far as standing. Taking a step forward was a whole other thing.

"Whoa, watch it there," he said, grabbing me around the middle as I stumbled into him. "Take it easy. Hey, watcha got here?"

His hand reached into my coat pocket and removed what I knew, even in my groggy state, would turn out to be the gun that killed Harold Gordell.

Chapter Five

"Hey, Lloyd," said Detective Stephen Gelb on the phone to Raymond, "we've got a friend of yours in here for weapons possession. Fella by the name of Ernie Lanier. He's been sayin' he wants to talk to you." He looked across the room at me as I sat in the holding cell. "Lloyd just groaned like you've been doin'."

He scratched the horseshoe of hair around his mostly bald head, then looped a thumb through his belt, which, like a dam after a week of rain, seemed to be losing the battle. "Okay, I'm sure he'll be glad to see you."

I'd been handcuffed and taken in the patrol car to Roosevelt Hospital Emergency Room, where my head had been X-rayed, the scrape on my cheek cleaned out, and a butterfly bandage applied to the cut on my scalp. It was determined that I had a slight concussion, so two Tylenols had been dispensed and I was officially declared fit to be jailed.

At the station, my keys, my little date book, and my one remaining "valuable," a cheap watch, had been taken by the sergeant at the front desk. I was escorted into the prisoner processing room, released temporarily from the cuffs to be fingerprinted, and front and side Polaroids were taken of me that made me look properly criminal. Then it was cuffs-on again, up those same stairs I'd climbed twelve hours earlier, through the detectives' squad room, and into the holding cell I'd been so happy to avoid that morning.

"So let me get this straight," Gelb said to me through the bars as I sat with my head in my hands waiting for the Tylenol to make the whangs! go away. "You're telling us that the gun we found on you was used in a homicide? We usually don't meet people this helpful."

"I just wanted you to be careful with it because there may be fingerprints on it," I said, stifling another groan. "Someone is trying to set me up."

"Now that's more like what we're used to hearing." He nodded toward the interview room. "Lloyd said you probably wouldn't behave like an asshole or give us any trouble if we let you sit in there and have coffee, instead of this cell. What do you think? And how's your head feeling?"

He was asking this, not out of compassion, but because they were supposed to make sure people with slight concussions didn't go comatose on them.

"I'm okay in here," I said. "At least I don't have to look at myself in the mirror."

That got a big laugh.

Raymond arrived twenty minutes later. He looked through the bars at me disgustedly.

"You do seem to get into it, don't you?"

"I really do. And I'm a fucking idiot. But you've still got to believe me; I'm a fucking idiot who didn't do it."

"Come on out of that cell and let's go in here," he said, indicating the interview room cum lounge. Gelb unlocked the cell door and I followed Raymond into the room.

"Can I call Annie? She doesn't know about this yet."

"In time," said Raymond as we sat down in our accustomed places. "Now, what were you doing on 52nd Street with a gun?"

"I was only on 52nd Street with a gun after he put it in my pocket. Before that I was just on 52nd Street, looking for a job at a place I never heard of, and it turned out to be him."

"Was this the job the answering service took the night of the murder?"

"It sure was."

"You know, of course, this will mean nothing to anybody. You were on a deserted street, carrying the gun, and you got mugged. It might even make the *Daily News*, 'Mugger Brings Down Murderer.'"

"Ohh!" The whangs!, which had subsided in favor of a nice, steady throb, started to return. "I'd have to be an even bigger fucking idiot than I am now. Why would I be walking around with the gun? Why wouldn't I have thrown it in the Hudson River or something?"

He shook his head. "Saying you wouldn't have been that stupid is not a legal defense. You were found with what's going to turn out to be a murder weapon."

"But you believe me, don't you? You know I didn't kill Harold Gordell."

Raymond looked to the ceiling and gave a deep sigh.

"Unfortunately, I do."

We sat in silence. Something was eating at the back of my mind, the part that didn't throb. The flash vision of a gun butt coming down.

"He hit me over the head with the gun," I said.

"What makes you think so?"

"I turned my head and saw it at the last second. Just before it hit me."

"How do you know it was the same gun?"

"I don't, but it looked the same. Wooden grip revolver. If he hit me over the head with it, wouldn't there be traces of my hair or my scalp?"

"Maybe. And in fact, you might be lucky. I've got a buddy at Forensics and I think he's working late tonight. I'm gonna take some of your hair as a sample and bring it over, and we'll see if they found any trace evidence on the grip. This all assumes, of course, that he didn't mug you with one gun and frame you with another one."

"It's the only assumption I've got left," I said.

"All right," said Raymond, getting up, "this is going to take a few hours. Call your wife and then have some coffee. Enjoy the amenities."

After he left I called Annie, described the whole mess, and told her to go to bed and not to worry.

"Don't worry?" she practically yelled. "I'm not only going to worry, I'm coming down there to keep the vigil with you."

"Me and the vigil are going to try and sleep," I said. "It's okay honey, get some yourself; we're going to need it."

"Call me as soon as you know."

"I will. I love you."

I went back into the holding cell and lay down, but I didn't sleep. Maybe you shouldn't anyway after a slight concussion, but I couldn't stop thinking. He had no way of knowing a cop car was going to come along before I could recover and stagger away from there, maybe even find the gun myself and get rid of it. No, I wasn't supposed to get a slight concussion. He wanted me unconscious, or even dead. If I hadn't turned my head at the last second…

I must have slept a little, because the next thing I knew, sunlight was streaming through the smeary windows and I could hear Raymond's voice as he emerged from the stairwell.

"You'll be interested to know, my man, that either you conked yourself on the head with a gun, put it in your pocket, and hoped a cop would find you; or someone did it for you."

***

I called Annie on Raymond's phone, told her I'd be right home, and requested a western omelet, but Raymond held up a cautionary finger.

"Tell her not to break the eggs just yet. I need to ask you about a couple of things. Won't take long."

I passed it on, and Annie said she'd be waiting with an egg in each hand. I hung up and Raymond motioned for me to sit down beside his desk.

"The guys who picked you up said you kept saying, 'Did you see him?' Why did you think they saw him?"

"Because he must've still been on the block. It was just a few seconds between the time he left and the time they arrived."

"You sure? You were pretty groggy."

"I know I never lost consciousness. One of the things about writing jingles is, you get a feel for how many seconds are going by. After doing enough of them now, I can practically write you a thirty-second tune without a stopwatch. No more than twenty seconds went by. I'm sure of it."

Raymond studied me. "Okay, let's pretend you're right. Our guys are coming down 52nd toward Eleventh with a view of the whole street, and they don't see anybody. You're half-way down the block and it takes them, say, ten seconds to get to you. That leaves ten seconds for the guy to disappear."

"That's how it seems."

He thought for a moment. "What are you doing today?"

I remembered. "Oh shit, what is it, Thursday? I'm supposed to present something for Burger Meister, and I didn't write it yet."

"Life's a bitch, ain't it?" Raymond clucked his tongue. "Listen, you've got bigger fish to fry than those burgers. That gun was the kind of Saturday Night Special everyone and his mama has, and the serial number was filed off. So I don't expect to be able to trace it."

"He had that figured," I said. "He wouldn't have planted it on me if you could trace it. He had everything figured, didn't he?"

"Not everything," Raymond said with a grin. "He didn't figure on you still being around." Then he gave a big, loud laugh.

I didn't, because I didn't think it was meant as a compliment. Maybe it was a semi-compliment, but a good part of it was at my expense.

The memory of a loud crackling noise shoved its way past my headache. It was a sound from my Generation Gap days, of static from an elusive short circuit in my bass amp. The techies would assure me they'd found the problem and fixed it. Then we'd discover to the contrary. The sound would burst forth, ugly and uninvited, at any time, in front of thousands of people and at the very height of a show, like a stink bomb in the middle of a celebration. It drove me beyond ballistic.

Up until that moment, all I'd been feeling was relief, but Raymond's joke made me realize it went deeper. So deep, in fact, that I could almost hear that brain-frying *craack!*

He may be kidding, I thought, *but I'm not. Whoever this motherfucker is, he doesn't just have the cops to deal with. He's got me.*

***

I could smell the western omelet as I walked through the door. Annie came out of the kitchen, and we kissed the long, sweet kiss I thought we'd never kiss again, except on either side of bulletproof glass. She winced at my cheek.

"He didn't do this to me. I did it to myself against the brick wall, but it was worth it. That's how I saw the gun, and it's why I wasn't knocked out."

"Oh honey, your head," she said, gently touching my butterfly bandage.

"It's a lot better than it was. Raymond thinks they're not going to be able to trace the gun."

"Well, come on into the kitchen and have some breakfast. I went over to Murray's Sturgeon Shop and got some nova and bagels to go with the omelet."

"Mm, an eastern western. Speaking of lox, we've got to get a loxsmith."

"Already called one, and he's coming over later with some serious lockage."

I sat down at the table and dug in. The cats, ignoring their overflowing food dishes, sat on the floor to either side of me looking up at the nova, their noses twitching.

"Okay," I said, between forkfuls, "a few things about this don't make sense. For instance, why didn't he plant the gun here at the same time he planted the picture?"

She gave it a minute. "Maybe he didn't have time. The cats were flipping out, and they were obviously loud enough for at least one neighbor to hear."

"And that's why he put it under the couch cushion, not someplace subtler, but there's another thing: He called in the phony job the night before. If he knew he was going to break into our apartment the next day and plant the evidence, why go through the trouble?"

"Because he didn't know at the time that he'd be doing it."

"Right," I said. "The opportunity came to him later. And when he couldn't leave the gun, he went back to Plan A."

Annie gave me a skeptical look. "Plan A was to mug you and leave both the gun *and* the Nixon picture in your pocket?"

"No," I said, "that would be overkill. I think he stole the picture just for effect. He didn't mean to plant it anywhere until he decided to do the break-in. And I don't think he watched our place all that time, either. There was some other way he knew we weren't going to be home."

I took a big bite out of the bagel and lox, appreciating that Murray's Sturgeon Shop doesn't cater to prisons.

"Incidentally, I found out something from Judy yesterday about Gordell and Stan Hook's sister."

"Incidentally," Annie said, "I found out something from Dawn yesterday about Gordell and Phil and Judy."

"Really?"

"Really. When Phil and Judy first started going together they tried to keep it a secret from everyone in the business, naturally. But Phil was doing a lot of work for Harold at the time, and I guess he must have noticed how they behaved together on sessions. Supposedly, Harold told Phil he knew about them and it was fine with him. He even said he'd personally make sure none of the houses he did business with stopped hiring Judy as a result."

"Sounds pretty decent, for Gordell."

"Well, it was a pretty decent amount of bullshit. It turns out that, years ago, Judy sang for Harold on a demo for one of his prospective smash hit Broadway musicals. She did it as a favor, working for practically nothing and singing a lot of different parts. When the show went into the dumper, Gordell blamed it on her because she didn't do justice to the brilliance of his songs. But she never knew it until years later, when he saw his chance to get back at her. He not only told everyone about her and Phil, but he personally made sure they wouldn't hire her, even if they wanted to. And he eventually stopped giving business to Phil, which is a major reason why they're struggling."

"How did Dawn find out about this?"

"I don't how Dawn finds out about anything," said Annie. "I guess she works for so many people, she hears things. What happened to Hook's sister?"

"Gordell once humiliated her on a session, and later that night, she killed herself."

"He was some piece of work, our Harold."

"Definitely. Finding people who hated him doesn't seem to be the problem. The real trick is figuring out who's got it in for me, because someone sure does."

Annie gave me an anxious look as she cleared away the dishes and stacked them in the dishwasher.

"Maybe you should stay home today, tell everyone you're sick, watch the guy put in the locks. This is getting scary."

"I'm not staying home," I said as that crackling sound flashed through my mind again. "If I stay home today, I might as well stay home tomorrow and forever, and I can't do that." I noticed the kitchen clock. "And it looks like I've got one hour to write a fucking Burger Meister jingle."

"Well, schedule a shower in there somewhere," she advised, "so you don't go in smelling like a jail cell."

I did as she suggested and then, trying to clear my head, took out my guitar and the lyrics and got started. Believe it or not, I actually didn't mind being told to write disco folk songs that were not too Beach Boys. All it meant was that they didn't have any idea what they wanted, and if I could come up with something decent, maybe it would work. Or not.

I gave it my best shot for the time allotted, wrote it out, and started zipping up my guitar and my backup bass into their bags. Annie came into the room with the mail, looking at a session payment check.

"Well, I see again where I thought I was singing in a group of four, but I was actually singing in a group of eight."

She was looking at the group-size category on the sheet attached to the check. Unlike the record business, where the big money is in the writing and publishing, the big money in the jingle business is in the singing. Writers, as Phil mentioned to me when he was thanking me for doing all those parts, don't get any money for a jingle unless they sell it. And even when they do, which isn't most of the time, they only get a creative fee of about one or two thousand. So why are we busting our asses, you'd say? Well, I'll tell you why we're in the hunt. If we sell it, we sing on it.

Sometime in the late '60s, the two performance unions, Screen Actors Guild and AFTRA got the advertising industry to admit that if they could make billions, the performers should at least make hundreds of thousands, or maybe a little more if they worked often enough. So, singers get residuals every time a commercial is played.

And because, as Judy and I demonstrated, few can be the voices of many, a shrewd person might figure you could hire a small number of singers, but claim on the contract that there were a couple more.

"I don't mind so much that Group Eight is a lower paying category," she said, detaching the check. "It's just that four extra on the contract seems a trifle greedy."

"Maybe it's their girlfriends," I said.

"Or their drug dealers."

We looked at each other. Traces of cocaine on Gordell's desk.

"Please be careful, honey," she said, moving closer and putting her arms around me.

I buried my face in her soft, honey brown hair. "I will," I murmured.

She whispered in my ear, "And kick ass up at Magnum Opus with that Burger Meister tune. It sounded real good."

I gave her a kiss, and then moved toward the door.

"They told me it should have grit, savvy, and hope," I said. "You think it does?"

"Never mind the tune," she said. "We're the ones who need all that."

***

There were two things I had to do before Magnum Opus, and one of them was to go to Fred Allenson's to hear about the "improvements for the worse" that the agency had made to the tune we'd be presenting. As I walked into the outer office, Julie, his secretary, looked up at me from behind her desk and gasped.

"Good God! What happened to your face?"

"You think I need a new razor?"

"I think you need a new left cheek."

Julie was a poised, slim, attractive woman in her late thirties. She'd been Fred's secretary for the past fifteen years, and some people thought she and Fred were lovers, a factor contributing to his divorce. "It's not true," he once told me. "I'm not her type. Wrong sex."

Fred came out of his office, looked at me, and grimaced.

"I can see I'm going to have a profound effect on people today," I said.

His expression was etched with concern. "Did you get mugged or something?"

"You got it exactly right," I said, divesting myself of my two instruments.

"Fucking city. What did they get?"

"My wallet and my bass."

"Fucking city."

I reached into the pocket of the guitar bag and took out the music I'd written for Niagara Falls Security Bank. Fred indicated the open doorway to his office.

"Come on in and I'll show you the new lyrics they gave me. And I guess you should bring the guitar."

I did so, and he settled behind his desk while I perched on the edge of one of the plush chairs across from him. One thing about playing the guitar, you can't do it in a chair that has arms. Fred slid the lyric sheet across to me.

"Read 'em and weep," he said. I read 'em:

As mighty as Niagara Falls
With all its strength and purity
Niagara Falls Security Bank
For that Falls sense of security

"Well, this is just perfect!" I said in exasperation. "It's nothing like the form or the meter of the old lyrics. What am I supposed to do with this?"

"Wait, wait," Fred said soothingly. "Don't start hemorrhaging; you look like you did enough of that already. Just play the chords and sing your melody with the old lyrics, one line at a time, and I'll show you how it can work."

I did as he told me, and after each line, he sang back to me the new lyrics that went with it. It stretched my melody around some corners, but, in a way, it fit. I thought of a couple of improvements here and there, but they were minor.

I always liked working for Fred. He was unflappable. No matter how crazy things got, with clients making wild and absurd changes at the last minute, he was the eye in the middle of the storm. If there was a rational solution to something, Fred found it. And if there wasn't, he took no crap. I had seen him walk away from writing assignments, something his slavish cohorts in the business would never dream of doing.

"Okay, so much for that," he said. "We're all set for tomorrow morning at nine to present to Melvin McIntyre. I spoke to him today and found out, incidentally, that he's inviting Bobby DiMango to compete against us."

"Bobby DiMango is freelance. He's not a jingle house."

"Melvin's inviting him anyway. This is a new one on me. You're not supposed to have competitions for cheap, local bank commercials. I was going to tell him to go fuck himself, but I knew you'd already written it and it wouldn't be fair. So I didn't, and that's when he told me about the new lyrics. Fucking business."

"Thank you, Fred," I said.

"Oh, hell, I didn't tell you so you could thank me. It's nothing."

He doodled abstractly on his pad.

"Let me ask you something," I said. "Wouldn't you think Bobby DiMango is taking a chance by accepting an invitation directly from an agency? He's a freelance writer, and if other jingle houses find out he's dealing directly with agencies, they'll regard him as competition."

"That's right, they will; and Bobby should know better. He's already gotten burned."

"He has?"

"Oh yes. You don't know the story?" Fred flipped the pencil onto the pad and leaned back. "When Bobby first started in the business, one of the first people he met was Harold, who was only an assistant music director at the time. Sort of like Melvin McIntyre was until yesterday. Anyway, Harold told Bobby he was inviting him to compete for Cojones Beer, but of course he had no authority to do that. Bobby, in all innocence, went ahead and wrote a tune and played it for Harold, who recorded him in his office and said he'd present it and let him know. A couple of days after that, he called him and said it had been shot down.

"So wasn't Bobby surprised a month later when he heard it on the air. Of course, Harold claimed he'd written it himself and had the copyright to show for it. Supposedly, Bobby never made a big deal about it because, first of all, he had no proof he was the composer and, second of all, he was trying to get into the business and didn't want to make waves. Especially waves he couldn't prove."

"You mean 'The man who has no fear drinks Cojones Beer'?"

"That's the one."

"That was a classic. It ran for years. With the guy on the horse, Cojones Jones."

"Yep."

"And everyone knows this?"

"Some people know it, some people suspect it. I just know I was surprised to hear Harold had written it. It didn't sound like anything he'd ever written before."

So, I thought, another member of the ever-growing Harold Gordell fan club. Fred reached over, peeled off the top page of his doodle pad, wadded it up, and tossed it into the wastebasket.

"Where are you off to now?" he asked.

"I'm playing bass on a session for Stan Hook, and then I'm presenting a tune up at Magnum Opus for Burger Meister."

"Ah, rarefied air." He smiled. "Good luck, I hope you get it. And after you do, I hope you'll still compete for me for bank commercials."

"Fred, I would compete for you for piggy bank commercials."

I stopped at Julie's desk on the way out and used her phone to call the answering service. They told me Detective Raymond had left a message for me to call him, which I immediately did.

"How're you doing, hero; how's your head?" he said. "Do you think you could come by here and look at something?"

Chapter Six

We sat at his desk. The place was much busier now than it had been last night or this morning. Gelb was gone and two detectives I hadn't seen before were sitting at the desks in front and behind, talking on the phone, while cops in uniform kept walking in and out. Raymond looked tired. I had assumed he'd grabbed some sleep while his friend at Forensics was running the tests, but maybe he hadn't.

"Did you get those locks changed yet?" he asked me.

"Annie's working on it. There may be a locksmith over there as we speak." I pulled my instruments closer to me, trying to find a place for them that wasn't either in the aisle or up against the wood-warping radiator.

"Good," he said. "Not so good is the fact that there were no other identifiable prints on either the gun or the picture. We did, however, find out who rents the warehouses on that block where you had your little adventure. If the perp disappeared off the street in ten seconds like you claim, he might've gone inside one of them."

He reached into a drawer and drew out a piece of paper, which he handed to me. It was a list of seven names:

National Imports
Corrigan Plastics
Belvedere Communications Systems
Blank Paper Products, Inc.
Pelican Crystal
Global Exports
Spar Industries, Inc.

None of them seemed familiar in the least. But something about them activated the part of my brain that controls the silliness function.

"You know," I said, "I could write a jingle with these seven names."

"Is that so?"

"Yeah, check this out." I looked at the paper and did some arranging in my mind. "The words would be:

National, Corrigan, Belvedere, Blank
Pelican, Global, and Spar
Just as you reckoned
It's West Fifty-second
That is the street where we are.

"I can see," said Raymond with a heavy dose of the facetious, "why they pay you the big bucks. Now aside from that, do you recognize any of them?"

"Not a one," I said seriously.

"Okay." He took the list away from me and put it back in the drawer. "We'll see what happens when we find out who signed the leases. Maybe one of those people will be someone you know." He yawned and stretched his arms straight up, looking like a bored weightlifter. "I assume you're going to be seeing a lot of the folks you work with in the next few days. Whoever this guy is, he was expecting you to be in jail by now. We don't know what he's going to do when he finds out you aren't."

I nodded soberly as the part of my brain that controls the silliness function clicked shut.

***

The offices of Hooks Unlimited took up the ninth floor of a building on West 48th. Stan had expanded his operation, as many jingle houses were doing, to include a recording studio that could be used for more than mere demos. His new, state-of-the-art, 32-track facility had a control room resembling the bridge of the Starship Enterprise. That's where I found him and Bobby DiMango after being told by his secretary to go right on in.

As I pushed open the heavy, soundproofed door and tried to negotiate my entrance without smashing my instruments into it, I could hear DiMango's Crummy-Cake demo coming through the speakers at semi-earsplitting volume. Evidently, it had taken a further step in the process and McIntyre had authorized the demoing of it with a full rhythm section. I wondered who the bass player was, and why he wasn't me. Stan and Bobby were listening raptly and didn't seem to notice my presence.

"Hey, guys, how's it going?" I called out, making them jump.

"Holy shit, man," said DiMango. "What happened to you?"

"Oh, hi, Ernie," said Stan Hook sheepishly, reaching for the master faders and sliding them down to zero, making the music disappear. "Sorry about this. We had to do it in a hurry, but if it goes final you'll definitely be involved in it."

"I appreciate that, Stan," I said, trying to keep my voice free of sarcasm. Generally, if you write something for a jingle house, but another writer's tune gets picked over yours, you're still on the final in some capacity. It's something that would go without saying.

"What happened to your face?" he asked. "Are you all right?"

"I got mugged for my wallet and my bass," I said, trying to gauge their reactions. At no time last night had I seen the guy; he could have been either of them.

DiMango looked at my cheek appraisingly. "Took your bass? Man, I thought having my keyboards delivered between studios was a pain in the ass, but I guess it beats having to walk around with your shit and getting it stolen."

Bobby was stocky, almost my height, and always in motion, even when he was sitting down. When he wasn't sitting down, he was either fidgeting or pacing and, right now, he was doing a little of both. He had round, wire-rimmed glasses and a hairstyle that was early Beatles, with geometrically perfect sideburns.

"So what do you think?" I threw out there as I unzipped my bass bag. "Who killed Harold?"

It was a real conversation stopper. Hook fumbled some of the sheet music he was holding, and DiMango seemed to develop a sudden interest in one of the faders on the console. He moved it silently up and down.

"Come on," I insisted, "we all know Harold wasn't Mother Teresa. Who do you think hated him the most?"

The pause that ensued would have passed a pregnancy test.

"Well, Ernie," DiMango said to the fader, "it's interesting you should ask, since you went off on him pretty good there on Monday."

"Not that he didn't deserve it," Hook interjected. "After what he did, I don't blame you for being pissed off."

"How pissed off do you think I was?" I asked him.

"Man, you should've seen the look in your eyes." DiMango turned from the console, his own eyes boring in on me. "You looked like you wanted to kill him."

"It's true," said Hook. "It was a little scary."

"You actually thought I wanted to kill him?"

"I didn't say that." Hook held up his hands in a *whoa!* manner. "I didn't think so at the time. But after he was killed, you've gotta admit—"

"Stan," I said, "can you honestly say that what Harold did to me was so evil that I would go back and kill him over it?"

"No," said Hook, "of course not." This was Stan at his balletic best. It was amazing to observe him at an agency meeting, pivoting and pirouetting, everybody's partner. "I mean, all Harold did was reject your tune."

"Hey, he did more than that," DiMango put in. "He insulted your talent as a songwriter. If anyone did that to me, I'd be ripshit too. And you wished him dead, right, Stan?"

"That's true, you did, Ernie," Hook said, nodding his head.

I wondered what would happen if Stan ever needed an operation and got two contradictory medical opinions. He'd probably ask one doctor to perform the operation and the other one to undo it.

"Would you be ripshit," I asked DiMango, "if someone stole a tune of yours and used it for a multimillion-dollar ad campaign?"

He looked at me narrowly. "What are you talking about?"

"Didn't Harold once steal a tune of yours and use it for Cojones Beer?"

"Where did you hear that? That's ridiculous."

"It never happened?"

"I don't know who starts these fucking stories, but no, it never happened."

I glanced over at Hook, who seemed uncomfortable that DiMango and I were arguing at such a fast pace. It was inconsiderate to argue without leaving him time to jump in and support both sides. I wondered how ripshit Stan might be at the person who gave his sister that final shove into her grave.

"Well, then, I apologize," I said to DiMango, feeling I'd reached the point of saturation in antagonizing him for now. I attempted to shift gears instead.

"Did you write what we're doing today, Bobby?" I asked as I put on my bass.

He measured me a moment, his John Lennon glasses glinting. Then he shrugged.

"Yeah, it's a tune for the new Warm Spring campaign. They're gonna be the official douche of the 1980 Olympics."

"All right!" I said. "Let's do it."

The session went normally from there on, with Hook playing drums, myself on bass, and DiMango on keyboards. Then I added an overdubbed guitar track.

Afterwards, I stopped by Hook's office to get a writing assignment from him for Quick Chix Chicken-Flavored Gum. We'd be doing the demo on Monday morning, Hook, DiMango, and I playing all the instrumental parts, as we'd just done, and now we needed to book three singers.

His office was a grand place, laden with Clio Awards and autographed pictures of celebrities who'd done voice-overs for him. I sat in the plush chair opposite his desk.

"How about Annie, Dawn, and Eileen Watkins?" I suggested.

"Great," said Hook. "And as an alternate, get Margie Burnett. Tell Carol out there what you want, and she'll call in the booking to the service. Hey, I'm sorry for Bobby's behavior in there. I never thought you had anything to do with Harold's death."

"Thanks, Stan, I know you didn't." I also knew that as soon as I left, he would apologize to DiMango for my behavior and tell him he was right to think I'd killed Gordell.

I stopped at the reception area and gave Carol the names Hook and I had discussed. Then I used her phone and called the answering service to see if there were any messages from Raymond. There weren't, but Dave Krulick had left word to call him at home.

He picked up on the second ring.

"Schwab's." This was his little joke. Schwab's was the famous drug store in Hollywood.

"You got my prescription ready, Lick?"

"Hey, it's fuckin' Ernie. Don't kid around about prescriptions unless you mean it. You coming to Mikell's tonight to see me?"

Of course, even if everything else hadn't happened, I'd have forgotten about it. I would've loved to see Krulick play with his trio, but Annie and I had become more stay-at-home types since we'd gotten off the road. Besides being sick of clubs, it was a change for us now to be running around separately for so much of the day. When we came home at night, we tended to stay there.

"Sure, Lick, we're gonna try and make it," I said diplomatically.

"Bullshit, you are. You and that little honey you live with are gonna jump in the sack and forget about old Dave workin' his ass off at Mikell's. Well, listen, man, I've got an inducement for you.

You come over and catch a set, and in between shows I'll give you a taste of something my man's bringing over here tonight. Now you can take it or leave it, that's cool. But I know you're gonna want a taste of something I know about Harold Gordell."

"You know something about Harold?"

"Sure do. A little something I overheard on Monday and I just now remembered. But I'm not gonna tell you until you plant that sexy woman in front of me for the first show and then you step into my office for a little treat."

"Oh, shit, Lick, don't screw around. I promise you, Annie and I will definitely be there tonight. And I'll keep you company on your little inhalation inspiration, I swear to God. But please don't play games with me. If you know something about Harold, tell me what it is."

"Nope. No dice, chief; nice try. See you at Mikell's. First set starts at nine sharp." He cackled and hung up.

"Fuck," I said, and looked up to discover Stan Hook, standing in the doorway. I don't know how much he'd heard, but I knew by the way he was looking at me that he'd heard enough.

Chapter Seven

I caught a cab crosstown to Magnum Opus. A rickshaw would have been faster, as would walking, but not with two instruments. In addition to the aggravating crawl of the traffic, there was the irritating, static-filled radio station the driver had on.

I'd often wondered why the sound of static drove me so nuts, and I realized that, to me, it symbolized helplessness. When my bass amp began to fart and crackle, it felt like some cosmic entity was twitting me, reminding me that, at its whim, it could make my life miserable, and there was nothing I could do about it.

People say there's no point in getting angry over what you can't do anything about, but I say that's why you *should* get angry. If I could've done something that moment when my amp betrayed me, I would've done it. The fact that I couldn't was what drove me up the wall.

In this case, there was something I could do. I politely asked the driver to either change the station or turn it off. He switched to what sounded like a soccer game in Spanish, which was a vast improvement.

We arrived just a couple of minutes late for my Burger Meister presentation. The three agency people were already sitting in George's office.

George gave me a brief dirty look for my tardiness, before smilingly introducing me to Arnold, a small, mustachioed man in his forties, nattily attired in gleaming oxblood loafers, charcoal grey slacks, a navy blue blazer and a rug; Sylvia, a young, pale, librarianesque woman in a severely tailored white blouse with a cameo brooch, whose eyes darted briefly to the side as she shook my hand; and Roman, a blond, athletic looking guy in his twenties, who smiled broadly at me as he gave me a firm one.

I got out my music and spread it on the coffee table in front of me, gave the guitar a brief tuning, and let 'em have it:

We give you the fries
We give you the shakes
The best chuck and round around
You know what we've got
We've got what it takes
Our meat is the higher ground
Burger Meister, Burger Love
Fish and fried chicken too
Burger Meister, Burger Love
We've got the hots for you

I whipped into the music that would go under the announcer, a slight variation of the melody, for the exact time mandated. Then a transition chord, a modulation up a half-step, and we were into the glorious repetition of the chorus, ending with a triumphant high note on "you!" 60 seconds, right on the money.

I looked up expectantly.

They were all staring at Arnold. He sat there with his eyes closed, a slightly pinched expression on his face. After a long, tense moment, his eyes popped open.

"Do you think we could hear it again?"

I certainly did, so I wound up my concentration and gave it another go.

The identical silence followed, with all eyes on Arnold. His were closed again, and he had the same pinched expression. The whole thing could have been on videotape.

He snapped them open, glanced from one of his assistants to the other and said, "I don't know; what do you think?"

They exchanged a brief, desperate glance. Then Sylvia cleared her throat.

"Um, I guess it wasn't exactly what I expected. There was a part there, I think on 'fish and fried chicken too,' where I wished the melody was the same as 'our meat is the higher ground' because I liked that part. But on the whole, I guess it was okay."

She looked at Roman, who furrowed his brow. "I wonder," he said, "if it has enough of a feel of broiling to it. There were parts of it that I thought sounded more like frying." He looked over and gave me a sort of half grin. "Bernie, would it be stupid to ask you to try something?"

"It's Ernie," George whispered.

"Sorry." Roman widened his smile, then returned to the furrowed brow. "See, when you sang 'we give you the fries,' that was all right. But it still sounded like frying when you sang 'the best chuck and round around,' and they don't fry their burgers, they broil them. If you could take what you sang on 'we give you the shakes,' which sounded a little like broiling even though it was shakes, but that was okay, and sing it on the 'chuck and round' line, would that be too hard?"

I looked to George, who merely looked back at me. If this were Fred, he would have stepped in immediately and done something, but this was George. He laid his white-haired head against the back of his oversized chair and waited, like a judge minus the robes.

"Okay," I said slowly, "let me just take a look at the music and see how I can do it."

I tried for a few seconds to figure out how to keep it from sounding ridiculous, but gave up. I decided to just sing the chuck and round line with the melody going down. The "give you the shakes" line went down. Maybe he thought "down" sounded like broiling.

"How about this?" I offered, and sang it for them.

"Now I don't like it as much," said Sylvia.

"Tell me, Ernie," said Arnold. The other two instantly locked onto him. "Could you show us how it would be if you split the difference?"

"Sure," I said, "just give me a moment."

I looked at the music, then arbitrarily changed three notes.

"All right, how does this sound?"

I sang the tune just as I had originally sung it.

A long silence followed, during which I pictured myself leaping up from the couch and doing a Jimi Hendrix, smashing the guitar against the floor and setting fire to it.

At last, Arnold nodded his head and smiled. "Sounds good to me."

The other two broke into big grins, as did George.

"And we can cut a thirty out of it without re-recording it?" he asked me.

"Two little snips will do it."

The door opened and Todd Winston popped his head in.

"How's it going, gang?" he asked, looking around the room. "Did Ernie, here, do right by you?"

They all nodded and made affirmative murmurings.

"I think we're in fine shape, Todd," said George.

"Terrific!" he said. "Wish I could stay and hear it, but I've got to dash. Reps are dashing young men, you know."

He winked, as I internally winced at the lameness of his pun. Then he gave a cheery wave and departed.

George thanked the agency people and told them that, if they'd like, there were sandwiches and coffee in the lounge. "Ernie and I will book the singers and musicians for the session tomorrow, and we'll see you then."

We all got up, shook hands, and they left. George looked at my cheek.

"Are you okay? That looks like it must have been painful."

"You should see what it did to the building," I said. "I got mugged. The guy got my wallet and my bass."

"Terrible. What this town needs is more cops. Well, let's see about tomorrow's session. Who did you have in mind for the solo?" He got out a notepad and prepared to write down names.

"I think, Brad Adonic."

Brad Adonic was a relatively new singer to the business, but he had quickly gotten very hot. He was a rock 'n roll stud with a hoarse, bluesy voice that turned women to liquid. I thought he would be perfect for this.

"Okay, how about the group? It should be three girls. Annie? Dawn?"

"Definitely Annie and Dawn. And me."

"Getting that old falsetto on the contract, eh?"

"Now you don't have to put me on in some other way."

"Oh, yes, nothing like saving a little money. You realize, of course, this is just the first step on the long road. I don't know how many other campaigns are competing against this one."

"Hope springs eternal."

"By the way," said George, "I noticed how you pulled that flim flam with the melody. Very slick."

"I'm a Burger Meister shyster," I said as I zipped up the guitar bag.

***

That evening, after Annie acquainted me with our three new locks and I'd filled her in on Krulick's phone call, we were on our way to Mikell's.

"You know the damnedest thing about it?" I said as we walked up West End Avenue toward 97th. "There's a part of me that wants to blow my nose with Dave Krulick."

Annie gave me a worried look. "That would be one of the stupidest things you could ever do. You know that, don't you?"

"With every fiber of my being. And what's weird is how I can be tempted when I don't even like the stuff. Can you imagine how somebody feels who's really into it?"

"I never believed it when they said it wasn't addictive. You just have to look at the way people act about it."

"Sometimes," I sighed, "I yearn for the days when doing drugs had a noble purpose."

"I married Timothy Leary," she said, looking up in exasperation at the stars.

As we bent our backs into the hill between 96th and 97th, something else occurred to me.

"With all this stuff going on, I forgot to ask if you talked to Dawn about what she said in the restaurant."

"I talked to her this morning. Things are really bad between her and Gerard, and it's not just that thing about the prenup. You have to promise never to let her know I told you about this."

"Wow, okay."

"She's been having an affair. It's been going on for a little over a month now. She sees him whenever Gerard is out of town or working late. She thinks she's in love with him, and she's scared about her career."

"Scared about her career?"

"That's just what I asked. She said it was a slip of the tongue, that she meant to say, scared about her emotions."

I took a few seconds to digest this while we made our way down 97th toward Columbus. I felt sorry for Dawn's predicament, and I felt bad for Gerard because I liked him, even though all he ever wanted to talk about was the Knicks. But they didn't have a killer focusing his attention on them, so I thought they were doing all right.

As we approached the club, we could see the sign out front for the Dave Krulick Trio. I was pleased to note that Raheem Washington was playing bass. He was a smooth, inventive player, and maybe if I watched his left hand closely enough, I could cop a little inventiveness. The drummer, Tony Trapani, was top-notch as well.

Mikell's was a long, high-ceilinged place with lousy acoustics, to tell the truth. The sound tended to bounce off the ceiling and reverberate around the walls, so the further back you got, the mushier it sounded. But it was a favorite spot for musicians to play because so many of them lived in the neighborhood. If you were clever, you got there early enough to sit down front.

We were not among the clever, as it turned out. It was a quarter to nine and the club was almost full.

"It's too bad," I said to Annie. "He wanted me to put you down front so he could make love to you with his eyes while he played."

She laughed. "He always keeps his eyes closed while he plays. If he ever opened them and looked at me I would consider it an honor."

We got settled in, then made our way to the bandstand to say hi to Washington and Trapani. They seemed concerned that Krulick hadn't arrived yet, with only fifteen minutes to go.

"Lick isn't exactly set to Greenwich Meridian time," I pointed out.

"True enough," said Raheem, "but he wanted us to get here early to discuss the set. We tried his phone a couple of times and it's busy."

"He's probably embroiled in the seduction of some teenager," said Annie.

We bullshitted a while about the new Chick Corea album, who's playing with whom, and this and that, and pretty soon it was almost a quarter after.

"Man," said Trapani, looking at his watch, "this is starting to get serious." He glanced across the room at the owner, who was looking back at him with an irritated expression.

"I'll tell you what," I said. "Lick lives only a couple of blocks away. Why don't Annie and I go over and see what's up while you guys do a duo holding action? You think the owner would go for it?"

"He doesn't have a choice at this point," Raheem said. "Yeah, why don't you and Annie do that, and I'll try and cool it with him."

We made sure we wouldn't lose our table, got our coats on, and set off for Krulick's apartment on 95th near Amsterdam.

"I don't like this," I said, as two police cars bombed by us, lights flashing, fishtailing into 95th Street as we approached the corner.

"I don't either," said Annie.

My stomach dropped when we saw two more police cars parked halfway down the block in front of Krulick's building. A cop intercepted us and told us to cross the street and keep the area clear. As we did, we noticed an elderly woman standing and staring numbly at the scene.

"Do you know what happened?" I asked, trying to keep the apprehension out of my voice.

"I called them because of the noise," she said. "The music was blaring, and I was banging on his door trying to get him to turn it down. He never played his music that loud before. Finally I called the police and they broke in. This is terrible. A murder, right in our building. Somebody shot that poor young musician, that nice, nice kid. I think his name was Cowlick."

Chapter Eight

"Lick wanted to tell me something about Gordell. He said his drug dealer was coming over…" When I finally got Raymond on the phone, the words were pouring out of me. I was practically yelling.

After that sickening moment outside Krulick's building, I only vaguely remember us walking back to Mikell's, telling Tony and Raheem, and watching them huddle with the owner, who finally announced to the crowd that Dave Krulick was taken ill and he'd be refunding the cover charge.

Looking over our shoulders many times, we made it home, latched our spiffy new locks, and I tried to call Raymond at the precinct house. He wasn't there, but Gelb said he'd call him at home and have him get back to us. Ten minutes later, he did.

"All right, take it easy," he said, making me aware of how crazed I must sound. "This happened in the 20th, but I'll see who's handling it over there and coordinate things. Now, what are you telling me? You talked to him on the phone today, and he said he knew something about Gordell?"

"He said he overheard something on Monday. He was teasing me with it to get me to come see him play."

"What was that about his drug dealer?"

"While he was screwing around with me, he said his man was coming over tonight."

"Sometime before he had to leave for the club."

"Right."

"His man didn't have to be the only one that showed up there, you know."

"But there was coke on Harold's desk, and I thought..."

"You thought maybe he wanted to tell you his dealer sold to Gordell," Raymond finished.

"And another thing: Stan Hook heard me. He came into the room just when I was asking Lick about Harold." A spasm of guilt twisted inside me.

"Well, that could mean something, or not. Now don't take this the wrong way, but do you know a lot of people who use cocaine?"

Instinctively, my old '60s guard went up. "Maybe," I said warily.

"I'm not interested in busting any of your friends," he reassured me. "I'm asking because, if there's a drug angle to this, it would help us to know who does what and buys from whom. Do you know any of that?"

The Roaring '60s began to fade into the distance. "I may be able to find out something," I told him. "I'm not big in the drug culture these days, but people don't seem to mind talking to me about it. I guess they think I'm some sort of pioneer."

"Well, happy trails," he said.

***

In the morning, after I watched Annie depart for her first job, a demo for Imp-u-Dent children's toothpaste, I packed up the guitar and bass and got ready to meet Fred at the place where it all began, Harold Gordell's office. While I did, I tried to think how I could unobtrusively sniff around the snorters.

A good chance would come later in the day at Magnum Opus, for the Burger Meister demo. Brad Adonic, the soloist, had one of the more well-known noses in the business. Also, Tony Trapani, Lick's drummer, would be on the session. I didn't know what his mood would be like so soon after the shock, but he was another one. I'd have to play it by ear.

I caught a cab to midtown, and before long, entered what was formerly Harold Gordell's, now Melvin McIntyre's, outer office. Hilda Kravitz gasped at the sight of me.

"Don't worry, I'm okay; I just got mugged. He only got my bass and a little money," I said quickly, anxious to get past the mandatories.

"Oh," she said. "But that wasn't it. It was just that when I saw you walk in, it brought it all back."

"It was terrible," I said.

"And I told them about that argument you had with Harold because I had to. But I know you could never do a thing like that."

"They'll catch the guy, Hilda, don't worry," I said.

"That's what I pray for. And I'm sorry they outlawed the death penalty."

She gazed down at her desk. "You know, they never appreciated Harold. He really was a wonderful man." She took a quick look at McIntyre's closed door. "It's only three days, but it's like Harold never existed here." Her voice got very soft. "I think Melvin's trying to…"

The door to the inner office opened, and out stepped Melvin McIntyre. He was dressed in a more expensive suit than before, but still looked like an overweight man with greasy hair and a moon-shaped head, to go with his lunar landscape complexion.

"Ah, Ernie, I see you're here. Is Fred with you?" He looked around, as if Fred might pop up from behind a couch.

"No, I guess I'm early. He should be here any minute."

As if on cue, the door opened and Fred entered, briskly unbuttoning his camel-hair coat.

"Melvin! How're you doing?" he said, giving him one of his more winning smiles, hand extended.

McIntyre gave him a rictus-like smile in return. "Hello, Fred," he said, taking the handshake loosely.

He indicated his office. "Why don't you both come in and play me what you've got for Niagara Falls Security? Is it a natural wonder?" He cocked his head slightly, as if saying "get it?"

"It'll send you over a barrel," I told him.

With a sweeping arm motion, he signaled us into the office.

The furniture was the same, but everything on the walls was different. Harold had Clio Awards and pictures of him with various celebrities. McIntyre's walls displayed artwork in the style of postimpressionist Ramada.

He sat down in the chair and waited, stroking his fingers along the desk, while I settled onto the sofa next to Fred, got out my music, and unpacked the guitar. I looked at the notes for a second, because the original tune was still in my mind, but it all came back, and I began.

When I got to the "falls sense of security" part, I held the note on "falls…" and paused to explain to McIntyre that there'd be layered vocal parts at this point, with the singers repeating the word, giving it a cascading effect. He nodded, and I continued into "…sense of security" and wrapped it up.

"Okay," he said neutrally, showing no reaction to the tune, "I was hoping the Creative group could come down here and listen to it, but they can't. So, what you can do is record it into my machine here…" He pointed to an ancient tape recorder on the shelf next to his desk. "I'll set it up."

I glanced over at Fred, who said, "Is Bobby DiMango going to do that too?"

"Bobby's scheduled for this afternoon," said McIntyre, starting to look through a stack of tape boxes. I guess that was his answer to the question.

A vein was beginning to stand out in Fred's neck.

"Well, why don't we come back this afternoon and present to them after Bobby? This is going to sound shitty in comparison to a live presentation."

"I don't think they have time for that." McIntyre selected a box containing someone's demo reel. "Here, we can record over this."

"I don't understand," said Fred. "They can listen to a live performance in the same time it takes to listen to a tape."

"No, it's faster this way. A lot of time gets taken up making introductions and being social, and so forth. This way I can tell them it'll be a short meeting, and they'll like that better."

You couldn't fight logic like that. I picked up my guitar and the music and trudged over to McIntyre's desk and the tape recorder.

"Go!" he said, and I sang the tune into the plastic microphone that came with the machine when it was originally purchased. I didn't bother to pause on the "falls" note and explain the effect; I just sang it straight through. Since he hadn't checked for volume levels, I could have sounded anywhere from distortingly loud on the tape, to inaudible.

"All right," he said. "Do you fellas want to hear it back?"

"You sure you've got the time for it?" said Fred.

"Oh, yes," McIntyre answered, quite seriously.

The phone rang.

McIntyre gave it a sour look and made no move to answer it. It rang again. He snatched it up.

"Yes?" he said. He listened for a few seconds, then began to shake his head, his eyes looking pained at whatever he was hearing. "Please. I'm telling you, don't worry about it." A pause. "I will, I will. Listen, this is kind of a bad time. Can we…? Okay. All right."

He put down the phone distractedly. Then he seemed to remember Fred and I were there.

"Oh, sorry," he said as he located the rewind button and, after accidentally allowing the tape to run off, threaded it back in and hit "Play."

It sounded like someone singing in a room with a hidden microphone. "I think that's fine," said McIntyre. "I'll show it to them later and let you know."

Fred gathered up his coat. "Melvin, this has been a rare experience. You are a worthy successor to Harold."

"Thanks," said McIntyre. "I know I have some big shoes to fill." He looked modestly down at the desk.

"Just keep shoving paper into the toes until you do," said Fred.

As we passed by Hilda on our way out, she looked up sadly. "'Bye, Ernie; see you next time."

It would have been nice if next time were right then, so she could finish what she was saying before McIntyre appeared. And maybe I could even find out something about that call. She'd put it straight through without asking him. The caller's voice was the first one he heard, not hers. But Fred was out the door, and there was no reason I could come up with for suddenly staying there.

He stood next to me in the hallway by the elevator, buttoning up his coat.

"Look, I'm really sorry about what happened in there," he said. "No, no, don't wave it off, I mean it. This business can be ridiculous sometimes, no matter how you try to prevent it."

"I'm sorry for you," I said. "Because you're getting screwed out of this account."

"Well, don't be sorry about that. Look at us, two sorry assholes." He laughed. "Boy, Hilda looked sorrier than both of us."

"I guess she was loyal to Harold, and she doesn't like McIntyre very much. She feels like she's on the spot."

"The opposite," he said, as the elevator arrived. "She's off the spot. Harold used to put her name on the singers' contracts, but now those days are over."

***

I cabbed it to Magnum Opus for the Burger Meister session. As I stepped out of the elevator, I saw George Magnus imparting what sounded like serious instructions to Tracy, the new receptionist. Tracy was a teenager with long, black hair and bangs that nearly covered her eyes. She was nodding earnestly every third word or so. George looked up.

"Ah! Here you are. Come with me."

I followed him to his office, and he showed me a writing assignment for a perfume called Eureka Cologne for Men.

"It's for a delightful lady named Minnie Sweet, over at TL&C. It's not due until Wednesday morning, and we don't even have to present it to her. We're just going to demo it and she'll be there for the session; isn't that nice? Now do me a favor: Don't just show up suddenly at the last second." He gave me a meaningful look, his bushy eyebrows lowering like storm clouds.

I proceeded to the studio and saw Tony Trapani unpacking his sticks in the drum booth. I stuck my head inside and we both looked at each other for a moment. "God, Traps," I said, "it's hard to believe."

He flexed his neck and shoulder muscles, something he did a lot of lately. "Whoever the motherfucker is who did this," he said, "I'd like to wrap my snares around his fucking throat." He stomped his right foot down hard on the bass drum pedal.

"I hear you," I said and then took the plunge. "Hey, let me ask you something." I dropped my voice several decibels. "Who was Lick getting his blow from?"

I hoped it wouldn't seem insensitive, that Tony would take it in a secret, fraternal way, as from a fellow worshiper of powder power.

He did. "Dunno," he said, as he tried out the crash cymbal. "Lick never told me. But it's someone in the jingle business, I know that. Lick used to say he was surprised to get such good shit from a jingle person. He didn't think jingle people were that hip." He gave me a slightly embarrassed grin. "Present company excluded, of course."

"I'm hip," I said, giving him a copy of the music.

I waved hello to George and the three clients behind the glass, plugged in my bass, and we began.

The instrumental track went smoothly, as I expected it would. Clients usually didn't comment during this phase, since many of them didn't know what they were hearing without the vocals. Many of them didn't know what they were hearing even with the vocals, but I always tried to contain my cynicism and assume they did. We recorded a couple of keyboard and guitar overdubs and wrapped it up. It was now star time, the solo by Brad Adonic.

Brad was waiting in the singers and musicians' lounge, slouched on the couch, idly playing with the tiny spoon that hung on a gold chain around his neck. He was talking on the phone.

"Well, tell Clive I don't know if I'll be at Elaine's tonight or not. If he's there and I'm there, we'll talk." He looked up and noticed me, giving me a slight wiggle of his fingers in salutation. "Tell him if he wants to hang around in case I get there, that's fine. Aside from that, I don't know. Listen, I've gotta go into a session now; I'll call you back later. Ciao."

He hung up the phone and stood up from the couch. "Ernie, my man, what's shakin', bacon?" He extended his hand in the power-to-the-people handshake we all used to give each other back in the revolutionary days and tossed his blond-tipped surfer's hair. "You have some kinda accident?" he asked, noticing my cheek.

"It's just a hickey," I said, grabbing his right hand and returning his clasp. "Let me take you in to meet your fans, and then I'll show you the tune."

"Epic," he said and followed me into the control room.

George and the agency people looked up as we entered. "Folks," I said to the threesome, "I'd like you to meet Brad Adonic. He's going to do the solo."

They all stood. Arnold nodded his head, Roman reached out and gave him an unrevolutionary jock handshake, and Sylvia blushed. They murmured variations of "pleased to meet you."

"Let's go out to the studio, and I'll show it to you," I said to Adonic. "We'll just be a minute," I said to the others.

A word here about Brad Adonic: He was a musical idiot savant. He couldn't find middle C on a piano if you painted it Day Glo, but if you sang him something once, he had it. And not only that, he had it better than you had it. His voice was that of a man in yearning need. It could hoarsely reach out for you and touch your soul, and then soar like a clarion trumpet. He had an endless repertoire of vocal twists and turns that he would apply along the way as he sang your melody, making your version of it seem bland by comparison.

I gave him the music, which he looked at only to read the words, and he stared fixedly at it as I sang the tune for him. When I'd finished, he continued to look at it for a couple of seconds longer, his eyes almost closed and his head bobbing gently up and down. Then it became a subtle side-to-side movement, as if he were on rewind. His eyes came fully open and he grinned at me.

"All right, dude! Heavy tune! Lemme hear the track."

I signaled Robbie the engineer to play the instrumental track. Adonic stepped over to the microphone and we both put on our headsets.

He began to sing. Fries and shakes never sounded so erotically desirable. He sang my melody at one point with a slight difference from the way I'd written it, but it was a better phrase, so I let it go. I chalked it up to his "edit" function.

"Great, Brad," I said. "Kick ass, man. I'm going into the booth."

I entered the control room to find the agency people all aflutter. I thought I saw Sylvia breathing hard. "How do you like it, so far?" I asked them.

"That guy's terrific!" Roman enthused. "The whole thing is terrific. It doesn't even sound like it did when you sang it for us."

"Well, that's what we try to accomplish," I told him.

"It's really well produced," said Arnold, nodding his head sagely.

"Wow," said Sylvia.

I sat down next to Robbie, and we had Brad do several takes, saving all of them on other tracks. He varied them in subtle ways, and, on one, grunted before singing "we've got the hots for you," causing Sylvia to make a little noise.

During the final take, Todd Winston stuck his head inside the doorway and listened. As he did, his expression seemed to indicate he had something on his mind.

"Everything okay?" I asked him.

"Sounds fantastic," he said, flashing one of those confident smiles at the clients. Then at me. "Got a second, Ernie?"

"Sure," I said, getting up from my chair.

"We'll just be a moment," he told everyone as we stepped outside the control room door. Instantly, the smile vanished.

"Doesn't it sound like 'Good Tokes for Good Folks'?" he asked with concern. He was talking about one of the songs I'd recorded in the '60s with Generation Gap.

"Don't think so," I said, trying to imagine what he meant. The rhythmical feel was a bit similar, but the melody and chord changes were altogether different.

"The part about how their meat is the higher ground sounded just like 'pass that high around,'" he said, singing it to me.

He was right. When I put a melody to the line, it must have triggered a subconscious connection. It's funny how that works sometimes. George Harrison once wrote a hit song called "My Sweet Lord" that was "He's So Fine" by the Chiffons, practically note for note. He wound up paying for it too.

This wasn't the same. "It's only one bar of music tucked into the middle of the tune," I reassured him. "But nice catch. I didn't realize you were into Generation Gap."

"It was hard to get away from it," he said. "Seriously, you're sure this is okay? I don't want a major account to turn into a major lawsuit."

"It'll be fine," I said. "Besides, it would cost me too much money to sue myself."

The smile returned.

"True enough," he said. "Didn't mean to interrupt the session, but I needed to make sure we had an ass cover."

He gave me a pat on the shoulder, nodded, and moved on down the hallway.

I stepped back into the control room thinking that Winston had an advantage over a lot of other music reps in that he could actually hear music.

"Sorry for the delay," I said, slipping back into the chair. Robbie replayed the last take, and I turned to the clients. "I'd say we've got it, wouldn't you?"

They all nodded thoughtfully. If I told them we'd also be using parts of other Brad Adonic takes, it would have been an invitation to disaster. They would've wanted to stay for the mix, a flesh-crawling prospect.

I flipped the intercom, told Brad it was great, and that he should come in and hear it.

The agency people stared at him as he listened, his eyes closed and a half smile on his lips. "Yeah," he said when it was over. "Sounds cool."

Everyone gathered around him and gushed for a while, and then George announced that we had about twenty minutes before the backup singers arrived, so why didn't the three of them join him in the lounge?

I told Adonic I'd walk out with him. As soon as we were in the hallway, I gestured for him to come closer because I wanted to talk softly.

"Listen, man," I said, "do you know where there's some good blow around? I've been getting shit lately that's Johnson and Johnson Baby Powder."

His eyes lit up. "Fuck, man, sure I do. If we had time, we could go somewhere and I'd show it to you, but I've gotta get to the next gig. There's some fine shit around." He looked dreamy at the thought of it.

"There isn't enough of it around me," I said. "I have to expand my horizons."

"You know who's got some classic shit, Bobby DiMango. Great hash too. Are you into hash? Hell, stupid question, right?"

"I was into hash when you were into baby powder for real."

He cracked up and we both slapped palms. "Yeah," he said, as we headed toward the elevator, "check out my man Bobby." He punched the elevator button and smiled at Tracy, who looked down at her desk and giggled.

After Adonic departed, I didn't know how I was going to kill the next ten or fifteen minutes before Annie and Dawn arrived for the background vocals. Joining George and the clients in the lounge was not an option.

As I passed by the smaller studio where they did announcer voice-overs and mixes, I heard familiar music. It was the Arrogante underscore we'd done on Tuesday. I stuck my head inside and saw Paul, their other engineer, setting up a mix.

"Hey, Paul, what's doin'?" I said to his back, as he stuffed the ends of one cable after another into a panel with little holes in it called a patch bay, creating something that looked like rubber spaghetti.

"Oh, hi, Ernie," he said, looking up. "I'm setting up a mix for that Arrogante thing you played on. It's going final."

I stepped inside, closed the door and pulled up a chair, figuring this was as good a place to hang out as any, and Paul started the tape. A babble of voices and instruments issued from the speakers, followed by the arranger giving the count-off.

"God, you guys don't stop talking until the last possible second, do you?" Paul said, shaking his head. "You should have some pity on us poor engineers."

He ran it back and we heard it again. Suddenly, I sat bolt upright in the chair.

"Paul, can you run me off a quick cassette copy of all that noise before the count-off, so I can listen to it through headphones?"

"You're kidding."

"No, I'm dead serious. Do you mind? It should just take you a second."

"Hey, no prob," he said, shrugging. He patched in a couple of additional cables, popped a cassette into one of the machines, and played that portion of the tape again. I grabbed a set of headphones and plugged them into the jack on the cassette player.

I played it over and over. Amidst the jumble, Dave Krulick's voice could be clearly heard saying, "I've got a new man, and he's put me on the Grade A list."

The whole scene came back to me, my hurried attempt to tune the bass and check out the music at the same time, Krulick teasing me from the other side of the partition. I wasn't paying attention because I was concentrating on getting ready under pressure.

Did I say something back to him? I couldn't remember. I must have, because the next thing I heard on the tape sounded like him answering me. It was mixed in with all the honks and squeaks and was almost overlapped by the arranger beginning the count-off. On the bare, frustrating edge of audibility, I thought I heard him say, "'Cause my man's big Stan."

CHAPTER NINE

I asked Paul to make me a second cassette copy, which I intended to give to Raymond.

"Do you want a copy of the spot too, once it's mixed?" he asked. "Or is this some kind of footnote to advertising history?"

"It's a new concept. Some people release anthologies of their out-takes. I'm collecting all the moments in the studio when I didn't play at all."

He gave me a strange look as I stepped outside to discover that Annie and Dawn were here. So, after introductions to the clients, I took them and the vocal parts out to the studio to rehearse at the piano.

"Found something interesting; tell you later," I couldn't help saying to Annie as Dawn walked ahead of us.

She looked at me sideways and I shrugged.

We did our "girls' trio," my falsetto folding in with their voices. (I love doing that, I must confess.) Forty-five minutes later, we came into the control room.

Sylvia just couldn't get over it. "I just can't get over it," she said in wonder. "I thought after Brad got through, it couldn't possibly need any more." Arnold nodded in solemn agreement, and Roman stared at Dawn.

Dawn looked at her watch. "Oh my, I've got to fly. My next session is way across town. We're still on for dinner tonight?" she asked Annie and me.

"As on as always," said Annie.

"Great," said Dawn. "Nice meeting you all," she told the clients. "It's a wonderful spot. Good luck with it." And with that she was gone.

George beamed at the agency people. "Well, that's about it, except for the drudgery of the mix, and I'm sure you'd be bored with that. But when it's done, Ernie and Robbie will have it sounding even better than what you've just heard."

They each shook my hand again in their own special ways and departed, with George in their wake.

"What did you find out?" Annie said, as soon as we were alone out in the corridor.

"While I was plugging in for the Arrogante session, Lick was talking to me about his dealer. He said something just before the count-off that I didn't hear at the time, but the tape was rolling and it picked up."

"What did he say?"

I took out one of the cassettes. "Honey, I hate to do this to you, but I'm not telling you, because I don't know for sure. It's really hard to hear. I want you to listen to it first, and then tell me what you think."

"This is horrible of you. I have to leave in two minutes for another session, and I won't be able to listen till I get home. The suspense will be unbearable."

"I'm unbearably sorry," I said, "but I don't want to influence you. It's like those old rock 'n roll misinterpretations: Jimi Hendrix singing ''Scuse me while I kiss this guy.' Once you hear it that way it sticks in your brain."

"Okay," she sighed, "I'll listen to it with an unsticky brain."

We kissed good-bye and I went back into the booth to mix the Burger Meister demo. We had some fun playing with the different takes Adonic had done, but the rest was pretty straightforward. After we wrapped it up, I called the answering service. There was still nothing from Raymond, but Fred Allenson had left a message to call him.

"Well, my good friend," he said, his voice practically jumping out of the phone, "you did something I've never seen in all my hundred years in this business. You beat out a live performance with a record-your-voice-machine demo."

"You're saying we got Niagara Falls?"

"I'm saying we swam up Niagara Falls. I couldn't believe it. McIntyre says the Creative group wants to meet with us Monday morning at nine; you okay?"

I did a quick flip through my little book and told him I was. And if I got there early, I thought, maybe I could have a little quality time with Hilda.

"McIntyre must really be pissed."

Fred sounded gleeful. I, not so gleeful, wondered if Bobby DiMango must really be pissed.

We talked some more about how stupid this business can be and hung up. Then I headed home to give that tape a listen or twelve.

***

"Can't quite make it out." Annie's eyes were focused in total concentration, her hands pressing the headphones tightly against her ears. "Could you take off some treble? The tape hiss is masking his voice."

Annie is nonpareil at hearing subtle things on records. When the Love Notes played bars for all those years, we constantly had to learn Top-40 songs for people to dance to. Annie could cop every part on a record to the very note.

I did as she asked and we listened yet again, my own headphones pressed against me like forceps.

"Nope, that doesn't help. Do we have a Dolby button on this thing?"

We did, but I'd used it only once. Dolby settings on home stereos were like a "Good/Shitty" button. When they were off it sounded good, when they were on it sounded shitty. I pushed it in and, for some reason, it helped.

"That's better," she said. "One more time."

I played it again.

"Okay." Annie took off her headphones. "It sounds like he's saying, ''Cause my man's big Stan,' but it's hard to tell because the drummer hits a cymbal on the word 'Stan,' so I'm not sure."

"There you go," I said, feeling very frustrated. "Maybe Raymond can analyze it."

We put it aside and started opening the mail Annie had brought in, but hadn't read in her haste to get to the tape.

"Now here's something different." She was examining the payment stub attached to a check. "This is a new talent payment company, and instead of just giving the number of people on the contract, it lists them individually."

"You mean the people added to the contract are actually named?"

"Well, at least their corporations."

Ah, and what does she mean by that?

It so happened that many singers and others who were making money in the jingle business were advised by their accountants to incorporate themselves. They would then be able to put a lot of that money in retirement accounts and defer paying taxes on it. So instead of a payment check to, say, Dawn Mitchell, with personal taxes deducted, it was made out to Dawn's Early Light Music, which was her "corporation." She was literally a one-person company hiring herself to perform the services she was paid for. Everyone had a corporation. Even Annie and I had corporations.

I swung around to sit next to her and looked over her shoulder. There was Annietunes Inc., along with five other names. Dawn wasn't on this one, but I recognized several others, including the writer and the jingle house. That accounted for five of the six. The other was someone whose corporation was named Boom Box, Inc.

"That must be who the agency put on it," I said.

"At least it's just one this time." She shook her head. "God, my ears are ringing. I have to say, though, it did sound like he was saying 'big Stan.'"

"I keep remembering Hook's face when he overheard me. But it's strange that Lick would say it was him. Stan never seemed like the cocaine type. Speaking of which, though, I pretended to get all druggy with Adonic this morning, and he told me DiMango deals."

"Well, Lick certainly wasn't saying 'DiMango'," Annie sighed. "Seems like the more we find out, the less we know."

***

We took a cab across Central Park to the East-Side restaurant where we were supposed to meet Dawn and Gerard. "What's the name of this place, again?" I asked Annie as we crawled our way through the 86th Street transverse.

"It's a new Italian restaurant, Fontana di Trendi."

"We ought to have them over to our place. You cook better than half of these joints, and it would be a lot less expensive."

"No, it wouldn't. I'd have to turn down jobs all that day to stay home and cook."

We arrived to find Dawn sitting by herself, sipping a gin and tonic at a table for four.

"Hi, guys," she said as we approached. "Gerard is stuck at the office all night so it's just me, I'm afraid."

"You will be more than sufficient," I said, feeling slightly grateful. The Knicks were hard enough to watch these days without having to talk about them.

Annie and I ordered wine as Dawn finished her G&T. She ordered another, then asked me about the very thing I was not supposed to reveal. "Did Annie tell you what I told her the other day?"

The fact that I was stricken dumb went without notice as Dawn continued.

"I've never felt further apart from Gerard since I've known him. I was so young when I met him and I didn't realize how little we really have in common. And I've changed since then."

"People do," I said, "especially between their teens and twenties."

"I've been searching my conscience." The waitress brought over her refill, and Dawn took a long sip of it. "It's not the money. You'd think when two people have been living together for ten years they would have something to talk about, but we don't. He doesn't care about music or the business I'm in. He's so absorbed in his cases, we hardly see each other." She took another sip. "I know I talk too much. I don't want to go on and on about me all night. What about you, Ernie? You wrote the Quick Chix demo I'm doing Monday, didn't you?"

It reminded me of the old line *Let's talk about you. What do you think of my dress?* but more interesting was how she knew that.

"Actually, I didn't write it yet," I said, "but I'm amazed at you. You have mysterious wellsprings of knowledge."

Dawn blushed, making her, for the moment, a study in crimson and copper. "I don't know everything."

"How did you know that particular thing?"

She looked at me coquettishly. "Maybe I'm a femme fatale," she said. Then her usual guileless look returned. "It's no great trick. Stan told me today when I was over there."

"How do you feel about him?" Annie asked, as the waitress arrived to take our orders. We told her we needed a few more minutes.

"How do you mean?" asked Dawn.

"His chameleonlike personality. Do you ever wonder what he really thinks?"

"I know what he thinks when he looks at me sometimes. It's creepy."

"Judy used practically the same word," I said. "You think he's into coke?"

"Hard to tell. He's not full of himself like most of those people. In fact, he's full of whoever he happens to be with. But he sure is hyper enough."

We perused the menus awhile and then ordered dinner. It was very nice at half the price and adequate otherwise. We were contemplating dessert when Annie mentioned the new talent payment company that listed the corporations. Dawn's eyes brightened.

"Isn't that fascinating? We'll get to find out who's being put on the contracts."

"Well, almost," said Annie. "We'd have to know who goes with what corporation. Did you ever hear of something called Boom Box, Inc.?"

"Where did I see that before? Why does it sound familiar? Wait a minute." She dug into her purse and came out with a check similar to the one Annie had gotten. "Here it is, Boom Box, Inc." She showed it to us.

"It's for the same agency," Annie said, "AT&M."

"This is fun," said Dawn. "It's like figuring out a mystery."

"My life's work," I said.

We had dessert and coffee and, shortly after, we stood outside the restaurant in the crisp, East-Side air, looking for cabs.

"It's only nine-thirty, Dawn," I said. "Why don't you come with us? We're going over to the New Yorker movie house to catch the ten o'clock show of 'The Deer Hunter.'"

"Thanks, but no thanks. I'm not in the mood for Vietnam. Actually, this is all working out perfectly; I'll be able to watch 'Dallas.'"

She looked at us both with affection.

"God, it's always so good to see you guys. I know I can be a drag, talking about all my conflicts."

"Not at all," I said. "We love conflicts. Why do you think we're seeing 'The Deer Hunter'?"

***

We came out of the New Yorker around one a.m. into a wind that, like the movie, smacked us in the face.

"I couldn't watch those Russian Roulette scenes," Annie said as we clutched each other and struggled down 89th Street, trying to move a wall of frigid air.

"As good an analogy for Vietnam as any," I said as the wind practically forced my words down my throat.

We got to our building, went down the two steps to our front door, just below street level, and stood there for a moment while I fumbled for the keys. I hadn't yet thrown out the old ones, so my key ring was overflowing. The key to the front door was somewhere in the middle.

"God, my hands are so cold, I can't even find the fucking key," I mumbled, feeling stupid. A car was coming slowly down the street, looking for a parking space.

"There's a dreamer for you," Annie said as my clumsiness continued. "Looking for a spot at one in the morning on a weekend."

And then she screamed.

I looked up as the window next to us seemed to explode. Popping sounds came from the street, and I saw pieces of brick leaping out of the wall near my head. We threw ourselves to the ground in opposite directions, my good cheek scraping painfully against one of the trash cans as I landed, but I was unaware of it.

All I was aware of as I fell was the sound of Annie's moan.

Chapter Ten

Silence. Except for the wind, faintly rattling the trash can as I lay in the dark with my face against it, and it was as if I had two minds at once. One was thinking: He doesn't know if he hit us. We're lying in a well, so he can't see us. He's sitting there deciding if he's going to come out and finish it. The other was thinking Annie, Annie, Annie, Annie.

I could feel the car's hulking presence just a few yards away (Annie), as I waited to hear the next sound. It would either be him driving away (Annie), or his footsteps approaching (Annie). But there was only the icy stillness.

I tried to stifle my breathing (Annie), which would have been gasps if I didn't use every ounce of self-control I had (Annie). *Drive away*, I thought. *Drive away, you fucking sonofabitch.* Nothing continued to happen every second (Annie).

At last, at long, long last, I could hear the car beginning to make its way down the block, and if you could detect reluctance in a car's sound, I thought I did.

I got to my knees and looked over toward her. She was still lying there, face down.

"Annie?" I whispered.

She rolled over and raised herself up on one arm. "Ouch!" she muttered. "I think I sprained my wrist." She looked across at me. "Are you okay, honey? Please tell me you're okay."

"You sprained your wrist!" I lifted her up into my arms. "That's the most wonderful thing I ever heard!"

My hands were shaking even more now, as I fumbled for the key, but we finally got inside and I called 911. Then I called Gelb, who called Raymond at home. Within a minute, the phone rang..

"Okay, glad you're all right," said Raymond. "You called 911?"

I told him I had, and that I'd described the car as best I could: a white, four-door sedan, whose only distinguishing feature was an outstretched arm with a gun at the end of it.

"Duly noted," he replied. "Now, in a few minutes a couple of the guys from the 20th will be showing up. Make them feel at home, and I'll be right over."

We were standing in the darkened living room, the chilly wind pouring in through the shattered window and the cats sniffing in rapt fascination at the dirt on our clothing.

"Got to cover that window somehow," Annie said, "or this place will be Nome Sweet Nome." We looked at her wrist, which was starting to swell.

"We should put ice on it," I said, "undesirable as it may sound."

Just then, "the guys from the 20th" pulled up outside, and I went out to meet them. I told the two cops about Raymond and showed them the window and the bullet holes in the building wall. I realized there was probably another one somewhere in our living room.

Raymond arrived a short time later, exchanged pleasantries with the two cops, and then herded us into the kitchen. It was far enough away not to be freezing yet. The cats followed, and I scooped them up, one under each arm, deposited them in the bedroom, and closed the door in their outraged faces.

I made coffee for us, while Annie sat at the table with some ice on her wrist. Raymond sat across from her.

"He's escalating," said Raymond. "He tried to frame you; now he's trying to kill you. Why would that be?"

"Who do I know that hates me that much?" I said. "Bobby DiMango lost out to me on a jingle today, but that's as stupid as me killing Harold over my tune. And it's a local bank jingle besides."

"Nobody hates Ernie," Annie said. "Only a psychopath would hate Ernie."

"Maybe," said Raymond. "But you thought Dave Krulick was killed in order to shut him up. Maybe he's trying to shut you up because you know something, or he thinks you do."

"Do I? It feels like I don't know anything. Just some stories about people in the business, stuff everyone knows."

Raymond cradled his coffee mug, brought it to his lips, and gently inhaled the steam for a moment before taking a sip.

"Doesn't really matter what his motive is. He definitely tried to kill you, and I don't think you should stay here tonight, or for quite a while. There's a hotel we use for witnesses we need to protect, and you could…"

I had an image of Annie and me, packing the cats and going off to stay in some hotel room, like we did for all those years in the bars on the road. It made me think of the jail cell.

How long would we have to stay there? That crackling sound came to mind, and I felt my familiar, instinctive rage against the idea of being helpless.

"I don't want to cringe in a hotel room," I interrupted him. "If this is about something I know, then maybe we're getting somewhere. We should be out there trying to find it."

I looked at Annie.

She looked back at me and I could feel her hesitation. Then she decided.

"I agree," she told Raymond. "Cringing is not good exercise."

"Thank you, honey."

Raymond looked to the ceiling.

"Do me a favor, then," he said. "Just cringe there for the weekend, okay? Think of it as a vacation."

It didn't seem like a bad idea, actually, seeing that the temperature in the kitchen was plummeting as we sat there.

"What about the window?" Annie asked.

"You can replace it on Monday. Nobody's gonna break in because of the iron grating outside,. After the guys get through tonight, we'll tape some plastic over it. Leave me the keys and I'll give them back to you tomorrow at the hotel. You should try and stay inside as much as you can."

"Speaking of taping," said Annie, "we have a little tape of our own for you."

"Right," I said. "I've got a cassette of Dave Krulick saying something to me about his dealer. It was just before a session and it sounds like he's saying 'My man's big Stan.'"

I stepped into the den, got it out of my bass bag, and brought it back into the kitchen.

"He's referring to Stan Hook?"

"We're not sure that's exactly what he's saying; it's hard to make out."

Raymond shrugged. "I'll give it to the audio lab and, meanwhile, we'll check up on the whereabouts of Mr. Hook." He slipped the cassette into his jacket pocket.

"And now, folks," he announced, just like a game show host, "let's get your weekend getaway started."

***

"So he thinks I know what I don't know I know."

"You could put a tune to that," said Annie.

We were sitting on the bed in Room 429 of the Brandish Arms Hotel. We'd taken my instruments with us, along with a few essentials and the cats. I looked around the room, which wasn't bad by second-rate hotel standards. It had a color TV, but no cable, and a picture on the wall that I thought I recognized from McIntyre's office. The bed seemed firm enough and, hopefully, we and the cats would be the only living things in it that night.

"I just realized something," I said. "I meant to call the answering service about that booking I got from Face the Music the night of the murder. It must've been taken by one of the night operators, and maybe she's on duty now."

I dialed the number and, after five rings, a tired voice answered. "Musicians and Singers Registry; good evening, or good morning." I realized it was after three a.m.

"Hi, this is Ernie Lanier. Who am I speaking to, please?"

"This is Janie," said the voice, still sounding tired. "There are no messages for you, Ernie."

"Hi, Janie. I wasn't really calling for messages. I wanted to know if you remember a booking that was called in on Monday night, for me to play bass on a demo for Face the Music."

Her voice instantly came awake. "You're the second person who asked me about that. A Detective Raymond was here and wanted to know the same thing." *Good old Raymond,* I thought. "It was kind of exciting. We've never had the cops up here before."

"What did you tell him?"

"That I was the one who took the call, he didn't leave his name, and that he asked for you and only you. I asked him if he had any alternates and he said no."

It figured. "Did he leave a phone number? You would've had to call him back after you spoke to me."

"He did, but I didn't have to call him back. He called me again a little later and I told him you'd accepted the job. I still have the number he left. I already told it to the detective; do you want it?"

"Sure." She gave it to me and I wrote it down. "What did he sound like?"

"Just a regular guy. He didn't lisp or stutter or anything. And his voice wasn't particularly high or low."

"No regional accent?"

"No, just a plain voice. What's this about, if you don't mind my asking?"

"They're cracking down on phony jingle houses," I improvised, and then had another thought. I covered the mouthpiece and looked over at Annie.

"Did the service ever call you about singing on my demo for Stan Hook on Monday?" She shook her head.

"I had a booking in progress," I said to Janie. "Singers for Quik Chix on Monday at noon at Hooks Unlimited. Did you fill it?"

"That was your booking? It was called in by Hooks Unlimited. Let me check.... Here it is; you've got Dawn Mitchell, Eileen Watkins, and Margie Burnett."

"Margie Burnett? She was an alternate. Annie was supposed to be first call."

"Well, I didn't take it. It was someone on the day shift. Looks like Gina's handwriting. Annie must have been unavailable."

"She was never called."

"Huh!" said Janie. "That's odd."

"Is Gina going to be working tomorrow?"

"Yes, she should be. Do you want me to leave a note for her?"

"No, that's okay. I'll speak to her tomorrow when I call in."

Annie put her hand on my arm to get my attention. "You should give her this number so they'll know where to reach us."

I shook my head no. "Okay, Janie, thanks for your help."

"Hey, it's nothing. I'm sorry about the mistake; Gina just must have screwed up. I hope it's not going to cause you any problems."

"No, it's all right. We can take care of it. Good night...or good morning, Janie."

I hung up and explained to Annie. "I didn't want them to have this number because I've suddenly gotten paranoid about our old reliable service. Remember, he knew we wouldn't be home for those couple of hours on Tuesday when he broke in? Well, who knows more about where we are and aren't than the answering service?"

After laying out an especially bountiful variety of cat food, we began our "vacation" with a nice, long, sleepless night.

***

We finally got tired of lying awake in bed at 11:30 and got up. I started to work on the Quik Chix jingle, planning to also work on the Eureka Cologne assignment for Magnum Opus, even though it wasn't due until Wednesday, just to get it out of the way.

"Why do you think the service didn't call me?" Annie wondered.

"It could've been an honest mistake, but there's something vaguely fishy about it. Stan Hook made it a point to ask me to book Margie Burnett as the alternate. It was the only time he suggested anyone, singer or musician."

"Margie's a good singer, but sort of older-generation," Annie mused. "More Broadway and legit than pop music."

"Well, when I see her Monday at the session, I'll have a little talk with her."

I resumed my labors while Annie went down to the lobby to get the paper, but I found myself unable to concentrate until she got back. She finally did with a *Daily News*, sat down on the bed, and began thumbing through the pages while abstractly moving Pyewacket aside with every turn. Pyewacket, refusing to take the hint, kept settling down on each open page.

"There's nothing here about a shooting last night. So if he's reading the papers to see if he got us, he won't find anything."

"That's not good," I said. "If we'd been killed, it would've been all over the papers, even in the headlines. A double murder in a nice neighborhood like ours would be big-time grist for the paper mill."

"So he knows we're still alive."

"Yeah," I said grimly, "he does."

The Quik Chix spot was only a 30-second one, but I was having trouble with it. Fortunately, breakfast arrived at the door just at the point when I was really getting frustrated, so I had an excuse to put it aside.

"Okay," I said, as we gamely worked our way through two rubbery western omelets, "the day shift must be in full swing by now, so let's call the answering service after we endure breakfast."

Annie took a sip of her luke-warm coffee and looked at me with a wicked gleam in her eye. “Do you feel adventurous?”

“Why?” I asked suspiciously, trying to ignore the fact that my orange juice tasted like melted orange candy.

“Because I’ve got an idea. We’re only a couple of blocks away from the answering service. Haven’t you ever wanted to meet the faces behind the voices?”

“You mean we should just stroll outside and walk over there in broad daylight?”

“No, nothing like that. I was thinking more along the lines of bundling up in our hoods and scarves, like two good little secret witnesses, jumping in a cab right outside the hotel, and checking out Gina. What do you say?”

Chapter Eleven

Musicians and Singers Registry was on 46th, west of Tenth Avenue. It turned out to be a one-room "office" on the first floor of a residential building. After being buzzed in, we walked down a long, dimly lit corridor to the rear. A small, wooden sign saying Musicians and Singers Registry adorned what would otherwise have been an apartment door.

We rang the bell, and it opened a crack. Half the face of a woman appeared.

"Yes?" she said, looking us up and down. "Can I help you?"

"We're Ernie Lanier and Annie Sands," I told her.

"Wow, Ernie and Annie!" She pulled the door open all the way. "So that's what you look like! I'm the famous Gloria you been talkin' to for the last three years. How're you doin'? Come on in and meet the girls. Wow, Ernie and Annie!"

The famous Gloria was a short, chunky woman in her thirties with Clairol-red hair and lipstick of the same shade. She stepped aside and bade us enter a small room, dominated by a long table with a vertical partition running down the center. Two women sat, one to either side of it, only their heads visible to each other above the partition. In front of each was a phone with several extension buttons, quiet now, presumably because it was Saturday.

One woman looked to be in her fifties, wearing a beige cardigan sweater. She was almost painfully thin, with washed out hair and watery eyes. Gloria introduced her to us as Lois.

The woman opposite her was almost painfully fat. She looked like she was in her twenties, though it was hard to tell, with short, dark hair and small, dark eyes. This was Gina.

The divider was a sort of bulletin board with large charts tacked up on it, the singers' names on one side and the musicians' on the other.

"Did you bring any pictures?" Lois wanted to know. I noticed there were a couple of 8x10 glossies on the wall, one of which was of Brad Adonic. Jingle singers usually didn't have publicity pictures unless their careers extended past the studio. After all, if nobody sees you on the commercials, why do you need publicity pictures? Adonic's aspirations, however, went well beyond the jingle business.

"We have some old Love Notes pictures at home," Annie said. "If you'd like, we'll send you one."

I thought Gloria would have a coronary. "The Love Notes! You were in the Love Notes? Oh my God, they were my favorites! 'Promises at the Prom,' 'Why Don't Your Parents Like Me?' I used to dance in the kitchen to those songs. I'd do the Lindy with the refrigerator handle as my partner. That was you? Oh, I'm dying!"

"Well, we got lucky, that's all," said Annie. She glanced at Adonic's face on the wall. "Did Brad come by here with his picture?"

Gina laughed. "We wish!"

Lois explained: "His publicity agent sent us one. I guess we were on some kind of list."

"Can we make you some coffee or tea?" Gloria asked, gesturing toward a two-burner hotplate in the corner.

"No, thanks," I said. "Actually we can't stay very long. We came by because we wanted to talk to Gina about something."

Gina looked up in surprise, her eyes darting from Annie to me and back to Annie.

"It's nothing to be concerned about," I said. "Probably just a little misunderstanding, but we've always wanted to meet you all, so we thought we'd come down and say hi and clear it up at the same time. Is there anyplace we can talk privately?" I knew the answer to that one. Either the bathroom or the hallway.

"I guess you can go out in the hallway," Gloria said. "Is everything all right?"

"Yes, yes," we both assured her. It was awkward doing it this way, but I couldn't see another way. Gina followed us out into the hall and I quietly closed the door behind us.

"Gina," Annie said, "did you handle a booking for Hooks Unlimited for this Monday at noon?"

It was as if she'd told Gina we knew she killed her mother. She burst into sobbing tears, wringing her hands and keening, "I'm sorry, I'm sorry."

It startled us both. "Please," said Annie, "don't cry. We don't want to get you in trouble; we just wondered what happened."

She seemed to have difficulty breathing. We waited, while she got herself under control and took a crumpled tissue from her dress pocket. She blotted her eyes.

"I didn't mean it against you, Annie. It's something I do sometimes for Margie Burnett."

"You mean, when Margie is an alternate, you pass over one of the first-call singers and call her instead?"

"Yes," said Gina, miserably. "It just happened to be you this time. I could've picked Dawn or the other one, Eileen, just as easy." She started crying again.

"How much does she pay you to do this?" I asked.

"A hundred dollars each time," she sniffled, her eyes downcast.

I thought about it. "Margie must really trust you."

She looked up at me warily. "What do you mean?"

"Sometimes Margie is first-call herself. How does she know the difference between when she gets a job legitimately and when you give it to her?"

Now she began to wail.

"Okay, okay," we said anxiously. People from other apartments could probably hear her, and the two women inside could definitely hear her.

"Don't worry; we're not out to get you." Annie reached into her coat pocket, pulling out some tissues of her own and giving them to her. "We just want you to help us."

The tears backed off to sniffles.

"Help you?"

"Just tell us something," I said. "Has anyone asked you or anyone else here where Annie and I were at any given time?"

She looked puzzled. "You mean, has anyone asked me where you were working?"

"Something like that," said Annie. "Where we were working, what times we were working."

She thought a moment and shook her head. "No, nobody asked me anything like that. I don't know about the others, but I could find out."

"Let me give you a number," I said, pulling out my little datebook and ripping out a blank page. I wrote down Raymond's number at the precinct. "If you find out that someone was asking about Annie and me, or if anyone ever calls you from a music house called Face the Music, you call this number and tell Detective Raymond."

She nodded and put it into her sweater pocket. Then she looked at Annie with glistening eyes. "I'm never gonna do it again, I swear."

"I hope you mean that," said Annie. "Now, let's go back in and we'll say good-bye to everybody. They must've heard you crying out here; what are you going to tell them?"

Gina glanced over at the door.

"No big deal. I'll say you happened to know my cousin, and you just told me he's dead."

She turned, opened the door, and walked nonchalantly ahead of us inside.

"She's good," I said to Annie.

***

After another two-minute cab ride and a quick hustle through the lobby, hiding our faces and feeling like fools, we were back in the room and I was getting out the guitar to tackle Quick Chix again.

"Just a feeling," I said as I spread out the lyric sheet, "but I don't think the answering service had anything to do with him knowing we weren't home."

"Same feeling," said Annie. "If we could figure out how he knew, it seems like it would go a long way toward figuring out who he is."

The phone rang. It was Raymond calling from downstairs, and we told him to come on up. We hastily put the cats, whose reaction was predictable, in the bathroom.

The effect of Raymond in a small hotel room was impressive.

"Your friend Stan Hook seems to be away for the weekend," he said, "meaning that if he's our guy you either don't have to worry for the moment, or you do, because we don't know where he is." The cats started scratching on the inside of the bathroom door and complaining, providing us with a percussive, whiny underscore.

"I went by your place again this morning," he continued, "just to make sure we didn't miss anything last night. By the way, none of your neighbors saw anything."

"I'm not surprised," I said. "Most of them were asleep, and it was so cold last night that no one was on the street. This guy knows how to pick his spots."

"So far," said Raymond. "Anyway, here are your keys, and I took the liberty of opening your mailbox." He handed me several envelopes, a couple of which looked checkular.

I glanced through them and noticed one from that new payment service. This time it was addressed to me, a check for a session I'd done two weeks earlier for Stan Hook (that name again).

"Excuse me for opening mail in front of you," I said, "but we noticed something interesting about checks from this new payment service."

For the first time since I'd been in the business, I ignored the dollar amount and my eye went straight to the payment stub and its list of corporations under the Group Singers section. There it was again, Boom Box, Inc.

"Oh, man," I said. "This is not only interesting, it's mega-interesting."

I showed it to Annie, briefly explaining to Raymond about singers' corporations, people being added to contracts, and how this new payment service was the first one to reveal who they were.

"Annie got one with Boom Box, Inc. on it and so did Dawn Mitchell. But since both sessions were for AT&M, we assumed Boom Box was someone who worked for that agency. Now this one is a commercial for FY& I, who are bitter rivals of AT&M. He can't be working for both of them. This is very strange."

Annie looked at the list. "I recognize everybody here, even Stan and Deliver, Inc., Stan's corporation when he wants to be separate from himself."

"Right," I said. "And so it can only mean one thing."

"Hold it a second," said Raymond. "Let me see if I understand this. People are put on the singers' contracts as rewards for other things, like writing or being the head of the jingle house. But the agencies add their own people to the contract too, as a reward for whatever they do. And everybody's a corporation. Do I have it so far?"

"You'll have it even farther than that in a minute," I said. "Check this out: Annie and I know everyone on this list except Boom Box. There are the six singers, including moi, who wrote it, and Stan Hook, who's the jingle house. In place of the ringer from the agency, we have Boom Box, Inc. Now who could that be? Not someone working for any agency, we've established that."

"And not anybody's girlfriend," said Annie. "We used to joke about them putting their girlfriends on the contract, but I don't think ad execs date corporations. And this corporation would have to be going out with two of them."

"He's not the writer, and he's not the jingle house selling them the music," I said. "Could he be selling something else?"

Raymond thought about this. "Certainly won't hurt to look into it. If it's a corporation, we should be able to get the name of whoever registered it, and we can ask the folks at those agencies a question or two. But first, let me ask you a question or two. If Boom Box turns out to be our man, it eliminates everyone else on the contract, including Stan Hook, doesn't it?"

"Not necessarily," said Annie. "Anybody can have more than one corporation. Like Stan and Deliver, Inc., for instance, which is different from Hooks Unlimited. People have been known to get themselves on contracts as two singers, if they can swing it. The only thing they have to worry about is the union finding out."

Raymond laughed. "This guy isn't worried about unions. Incidentally, I might be calling you Monday with some of the names behind the warehouses."

"You mean National, Corrigan, Belvedere, Blank, Pelican, Global, and Spar?" I said.

"You memorized them?" said Raymond, looking at me cockeyed.

"I never forget a lyric."

We filled him in on our little side trip to the answering service, which reminded me of the phone number the killer had given Janie.

"Oh yes, that phone number," said Raymond. "It doesn't exist."

Chapter Twelve

After Raymond's departure, we sprung the cats and I got back to Quik Chix, but I still couldn't concentrate. I kept imagining those people at AT&M and FY&I, and their reaction when Raymond showed up. Would someone talk, or would there be massive pleadings of ignorance? Either way, it would mean no more drug purchases from Boom Box. Would that piss him off even more? Once someone's trying to kill you, he's probably pissed off enough.

I was getting pissed off myself, because I couldn't come up with anything decent for a dumb 30-second spot.

"Why don't you let it go 'til tomorrow?" Annie suggested. "We're going to be spending the whole day in this room anyhow, and it'll give you something to do. Let's suffer through a room service dinner and then hit the hay early. I don't know about you, but I'm fairly wiped at this point."

"You're right," I said, putting the guitar aside and reaching for the menu. "How about hamburgers, french fries, salad, and a couple of Heinekens? They can't screw that up too bad." As it turned out, I was only right on the Heinekens.

After dinner we fell into bed and slept twelve solid hours. I dreamed my head was in a guillotine and Stan Hook was the executioner. The blade mustn't have been sharp enough, because he had to do it over and over. He'd pull the rope and I'd hear the sound of the blade swishing down toward me, followed by a dull, wet feeling. I awoke to find Velveeta licking the back of my neck.

Annie moved closer to me under the covers, her hands gently finding me. "What's that song that goes 'in the morning when you rise'?"

"I think it's an old shaving cream jingle," I said, kissing her and turning her onto her back. I pulled down the covers and marveled for the millionth time at the perfection of her body. Even after nine years of living with her, I still felt like a high school kid looking at a live Playboy centerfold. And Annie would've been Playmate of the Year.

"Well," she said, stretching languorously and driving me insane, "why don't we see how many arrangements of it we can remember?"

***

And so our Sunday began and continued, except for the times when we came up for air. We managed to do a few other things, like having another rubbery breakfast and feeding the cats. I knocked off the Quik Chix jingle, the melody coming miraculously to me two seconds after I'd picked up the guitar, and then had a similar epiphany with Eureka Cologne for Men. We sat naked on the bed like two flower children and sang Jefferson Airplane songs (Annie does Grace Slick like you wouldn't believe).

As it was getting dark, we began to contemplate one more room service assault on our digestive tracts. "Let's get out of here," I said. "Let's go home and make dinner. We're going to show up back in the world tomorrow anyway."

"Absolutely," said Annie. "Let's start getting our money's worth out of those locks."

***

We went home and nobody killed us, and now it was Monday morning, crisp and clear, with a temperature in the single digits. The sun would have been pouring shafts of light into our kitchen had we not had blinds and curtains covering every window in the house. Annie and I kissed good-bye, and as she began her wait for the window-repair guy, I cautiously left for Fred's and my meeting with McIntyre and the almighty Creative group. Before that, though, I wanted a word with Hilda.

She was alone at her desk in the outer office.

"How're things going?" I asked her. "I thought I'd never see you again."

"Now why would you say that?"

I looked over at McIntyre's closed door. "Is Melvin here?"

"Not yet. Why did you think you wouldn't see me? Did you think he wanted you to lose to Bobby DiMango?"

"I don't know," I said. "What do you think?"

"What do I think?" Her voice lowered. "I think he's measuring my butt for the boot."

"How do you know?"

Her voice got even softer. "He gives me instructions to put all calls through to him and not ask who's calling. He'll tell me he's going to be in a meeting, but he won't tell me where. He…"

The door opened and Fred blew in, red-nosed and rubbing his hands.

"Boy, windows are cracking out there," he said. "I'm still freezing, and this is supposed to be a thermal camel hair coat from a genuine thermal camel. Good morning Hilda. Hey there, Breaker of the Sound Barrier." He grinned widely and looked at me with faux admiration.

I looked back at him with faux humility. We settled into the same positions we were in on the morning we discovered Gordell's body, even down to Fred doing his cryptic crossword puzzle. So, I thought, Hilda didn't know who McIntyre's caller was. But why the secrecy?

"Well, he's late," she said. "Don't ask me why because I'm the last person to know anything."

At that very moment McIntyre walked in. He spotted Fred and me on the couch and stopped.

"Oh, right, I forgot," he said. "Niagara Falls Security Bank. The Creative group wanted me to get you up here today so they could meet you."

"Good morning, Melvin," Fred said. "And it's great to see you too."

"Sure, thanks, Fred." McIntyre took a key from his pocket and sidled toward his office door. "Why don't you give me a minute and I'll call them." He went inside and we could hear him talking on the phone. After a moment or two, he appeared in the doorway. "They'll be right down," he announced, sounding like the Pope delivering a blessing.

And so it came to pass. And they numbered three, as it is written that wise men and Creative groups shall be of that number. We were introduced to Samuel, a diminutive, fortyish man with goatee and glasses, in a black turtleneck and razor-pleated chinos; Amos, a kid in his early twenties with a Charles Manson beard, in a tie-dye shirt and jeans (he gave me a power-to-the-people handshake); and Joel, a fiftyish, tonsorially immaculate man in a three-piece suit.

"Joel's not with the Creative group," Samuel informed us, belying my Biblical analogy and explaining the suit. "He's with the Accounts group."

"I'm the guy who's gotta go in there with the tune," said Joel, making it sound like a line from "The Dirty Dozen."

There's a clear sociological distinction in advertising between the two groups. People in Creative think of people in Accounts as crude salesmen of the Creatives' art and talent, who only know how to ass-kiss clients. People in Accounts think of people in Creative as airheaded phonies. I, as a neutral observer, believe there's some truth to both sides.

They all sat down and McIntyre took up his station behind the desk.

"Ernie," said Amos, slouching in his chair, one hand resting on his studded black leather belt, "I really dug that 'falls' effect you put in there."

Wait a minute; was I crazy? I could have sworn I'd sung it straight through without trying to demonstrate the cascading vocal effect. What was he talking about?

"Thanks," I said tentatively.

"Yeah, it was cool," Amos observed, "kind of like 'Blue Jay Way' from 'Magical Mystery Tour.'"

"I never thought of it like that," I said.

"Well, it must have subconsciously influenced you."

Samuel plucked something invisible off his turtleneck and delicately crossed a leg. "I wonder if you could play it for us. We're trying to envision how it will look. Obviously, we're going to use a lot of shots of Niagara Falls, and then, of course, the bank, but we felt that if we heard the music live in the room, so to speak, it could open us up conceptually."

"Sure," I said, unzipping the guitar bag. I checked the tuning, spread out the music on the coffee table, and sang it for them.

Joel smiled, tapping his foot randomly. Amos looked like he was meditating. Samuel stared into space, moving his right hand slowly through the air, like a blind man painting a picture.

When I'd finished, Joel nodded to me and said, "Very pretty."

Samuel brought down his hand. "That definitely decided it for me. I'm not going to wait. I'm using the Maid of the Mist in the opening shot."

Amos frowned. "I guess I needed to hear the effect. The song is okay by itself, but I really couldn't get off because I missed hearing the effect."

I was powerless to respond. I was sure I hadn't tried to sing it on the tape. Was this a parallel universe?

"You know?" said Fred. "Why don't we give the tape a listen so Amos can hear it the way he heard it originally."

"Good idea," said Samuel. "Melvin, I think we gave it back to you. Do you have it here?"

"I think so," said McIntyre looking around his desk. He discovered the tape under a copy of *Advertising Age*. "Here we go. Let me set it up."

He brought it over to his relic of a tape recorder and methodically began to thread it through.

Amos leaned across and touched my knee. "I love the sound of these old machines. It's like hearing music under the same conditions as when rock 'n roll first began."

"I heard that Elvis's first session for Sun Records was done on a Wollensak," I said.

"No kidding."

By this time, McIntyre had succeeded in starting the tape. I listened once again to the surveillance-quality recording of myself. Running under the whole thing was a low, whooshing noise. McIntyre had put the microphone too close to the machine, so it had picked up the sound of the motor. What resulted was a kind of drone, slightly out of tune with what I was singing in the foreground.

"Yeah!" said Amos, clenching his fist. "Now I see the falls!"

I looked over for Fred's reaction. It was vintage.

"There you are," he told them. "Now, of course, we shouldn't use an effect like that through the entire thing. We should use maybe three seconds of it. Save it for a special moment, you can tell us when, and we'll fit it in."

"Maybe," said Samuel. "I'll have to re-envision it a little."

"Man, I could use more than three seconds," said Amos.

"Oh, but it's so special," Fred said reverently. "You have to delay it and then show it just a little, make people say 'God, what did they do just then?' And then take it away! They'll be hanging onto their sets, waiting to see the spot again."

Amos, looked petulant, running his fingers through his beard and breaking a few tangles in the process. "Well, I guess so," he said. "I guess I can live with it. But we have to really pick the shot for it, Samuel. It can't just be the Maid of the Mist shot. Even if you think people fantasize about their toy boats in the bathtub."

Samuel's face reddened. "We'll have a meeting later today about it."

"And I'll tell you what," said Fred. "We've got some even more incredible falls sounds in our library. This was only meant to be a sample."

"I don't want to lose that quality," Amos warned.

"No, no, not a chance. Say, as a matter of fact," Fred said to McIntyre, "what time tomorrow are we doing this?"

McIntyre consulted his calendar. "I have it penciled in at ten. Is everyone okay for that?"

"It's okay for me," said Joel, getting up from his chair, smiling benignly, and heading out the door. Samuel and Amos got up as well, checked their pocket date books, and then began arguing with each other over when they could have their meeting today. They paused long enough to look up and say good-bye to us as they bickered their way out.

As their voices trailed off in the outer office, McIntyre looked worriedly at Fred.

"Are you sure you have that sound? I didn't know what it was when I played it for them and they started going crazy, so I didn't say anything."

"Not to worry, Melvin, we can get some great falls sounds. And if they still want the genuine article, all you have to do is put the mike on top of your tape recorder, put a tape on, press record, and then don't move or make a noise for ten minutes. Bring it to the session and I'm sure we can cut three good seconds out of it."

For a moment, I wondered if Fred had finally gone too far. Whether he'd penetrated McIntyre's anti-sarcasm shield, the irony curtain he lived behind. McIntyre stared at the tape machine as if to visually measure Fred's sincerity.

"All right. But not for ten minutes," he said astutely.

"Whatever's comfortable," said Fred. "Now, where are we doing this and who are we getting to do it?"

"We're doing it at Wired Angel Studio. It's a new place that's opened on the fifteenth floor of this building, so I won't even have to bring a coat." He laughed as if he'd made a joke, then turned to me. "For the singers, you can get any three women you want. The men are going to be you, Bobby DiMango, and Brad Adonic."

"Brad Adonic?" I said. "Brad isn't a group singer." Asking for DiMango was proper; he had written the competing tune and should be compensated. But Adonic had done nothing to sell the tune and was the antithesis of a group singer. Group singers were people who could sight-read music and sing intricate harmony parts with great precision. Adonic was as you've seen him.

"Well, he's going to be a group singer tomorrow," said McIntyre. "For the musicians, we've got a budget for keyboards, guitar, bass, and drums, and you can book anyone you want there too." He looked at his watch. "Oh geez, I've got to get to a meeting about the new Krugerand campaign."

He escorted us to the outer office, closed and locked his door, and then excused himself, continuing on out.

"See?" said Hilda as Fred and I put on our coats. "I don't even know where he's going."

"He's going to a Krugerand meeting," I said. "It's the new campaign: South African Krugerands, for the Discriminating Investor."

Fred announced that he had to run back to his office because Julie was out, which was good news for me, since it would leave me alone with Hilda. I gave him the names of several musicians for the session and told him to book Annie, Dawn, and Eileen Watkins.

"Will do," he said. "I'll also audition some waterfalls. See you tomorrow at ten on fifteen." He blew a kiss to Hilda and blew out the door.

"As you were saying?" I said to her.

She leaned forward and assumed the same whispery manner as before. "He's a compulsive gambler. Harold used to catch him on the phone, betting on horses, ballgames, everything. Some of the guys here say he owes his bookie big time."

Getting Gordell's job certainly helped that problem out, I figured, and not just the higher salary. I was sure that our six-person group tomorrow would be at least eight on the contract, with McIntyre as one or two of the singers. And what was this thing with Brad Adonic?

"Strange people keep calling. I used to think of him as a harmless shnook, but now he kind of scares me. I'll be glad when I'm out of here."

I heard the door opening behind me and quickly leaned back, grabbing my two instrument bags.

"Is Melvin still here?" asked Samuel from the doorway, looking discouragedly at McIntyre's closed door.

"He went to a meeting," Hilda said.

"Damn," said Samuel, "I left a small tote bag in there with some important things in it that I need for a meeting later."

"Well, I'm afraid he locked the office."

"Damn," said Samuel again, as he stepped back into the hallway, closing the door behind him.

"I'll bet those things in the tote bag were really crucial," I said. "Probably the tugboat and the rubber duckie."

***

And now, the main event, I thought, as I got out of the elevator at Hooks Unlimited. Just as before, Carol told me to go on into the studio and, just as before, I surprised Hook and Bobby DiMango in the control room, listening to something.

It was an instrumental track, and when Hook noticed me, he killed the faders.

"Hi, Ernie," he said.

"Hey, man," said DiMango, almost snapping to attention.

"How're you doing, guys?" I said, putting down my instruments and shedding my coat. "Did you have a good weekend?"

"Great," said Hook. "Flew up to Syracuse to see my niece and nephew."

"How about you?" I asked DiMango. "Do anything special?"

"I had to work," he said cautiously. "Somebody called me and gave me a shot at something."

"Okay," said Hook, "I assume you two were brilliant as usual with Quik Chix. We've got the singers coming at twelve, so let's get started on the instrumental tracks."

We moved out to the studio and followed the usual procedure, with DiMango playing keyboards, Hook playing drums, and me playing bass and overdubbing a guitar part on both DiMango's tune and my own.

Dawn, Eileen Watkins, and Margie Burnett arrived on schedule, and we all gathered in the control room. Since my version was first, I passed out the music, asked the engineer to play the instrumental track, and sang it for them.

Every pack of Quik Chix
Ranks among your best picks
They're a hit no matter where you're from
Each stick's really some stick
Shaped just like a drumstick
Quik Chix, the Chicken-Flavored Gum

I left two seconds open at the end, as per instructions, so the announcer could say, "And now, new Barbecue flavor."

"Neat," said Dawn.

"Really nice," said Margie Burnett.

"Yum," said Eileen Watkins. "Makes me wanna bite into a thigh right now."

Eileen Watkins was, physically, nearly the female equivalent of Detective Lloyd Raymond. She was an amply proportioned Black woman with twinkling eyes, who was an outstanding gospel singer.

When she sang solo, she could make a tire sale sound like the second coming. To a group sound she brought exaltation. Her only problem in the business was a slightly attitudinal one. I once sang with her on a session for an industrial show, which pays a lot less than jingles and doesn't have residuals. At one point during the session, she indicated an especially high note on her music and said to the arranger, "Uh uh, honey. You ain't gettin' that note out of me for no fifty dollars."

We didn't have any such problems here. With Hook, DiMango, and me on the men's side of the mike, and the women sounding great on their side, we knocked off both spots in about an hour. Afterward, I asked Margie Burnett if I could have a word with her.

We stepped outside into the corridor. Margie was an earnest, middle-aged woman, with a face that always seemed to be saying 'yes, I see' to you as you talked to her. She'd been doing jingles since years before the big singers' contracts. Unfortunately for her, those years were her good ones. Her husband had died of cancer a short while ago. I felt rotten for what I was about to say.

"Annie and I were over at the answering service on Saturday, and we talked to Gina."

Margie's face went several shades whiter. "Oh?" she said, trying for offhandedness.

"What happened," I said, "was that I was the one who booked the singers for this date, not Stan Hook, and I'd booked you as an alternate with Annie as first call."

"My God!" said Margie. "So of course you knew they skipped over Annie and called me. Oh, this is terrible!"

"I don't want to make any trouble," I said. "I told Gina I wouldn't report it and I'm telling you the same thing. All I'm concerned about is whether this is part of something bigger. I need you to help me."

"Anything. Tell me what to do. God, I'm so embarrassed."

"Well, just answer a few questions. Stan Hook told me to put you down as the alternate. He didn't seem to care about anyone else I booked. Does he have something to do with your deal with Gina?"

"No. Nobody knew about it…until now."

"Did Gina ever put you ahead of someone on a job for Harold Gordell?"

"Yes, a few times. But the last time it happened, Harold kept looking at me in a funny way and it made me very antsy. I don't know if he suspected anything or not, but after that I told Gina not to do it on any more of his jobs. I was going to stop doing it anyway; it was too nerve-wracking. I can't tell you how mortified I am, Ernie. If this demo ever goes final, I'll say I can't do the session and you can put Annie back on it. And I'll send her the money I get for the demo. I just feel awful."

"Don't worry," I said, not knowing quite how I felt. I was sorry Margie lost her husband and that she was seeing her career wither, but she was stealing from other singers. "We won't tell anyone, but you have to stop doing it."

"I will. Thank you for not saying anything. I'm so ashamed of myself."

I said good-bye to her, went back into the control room, and found DiMango and the engineer getting ready for the mix.

"You're up first, man," said DiMango. "I'll just go somewhere and do something." He chuckled to himself and made his way out the door.

The engineer and I mixed my version and then I headed out, stopping to wave good-bye to Hook, who looked up from behind his desk, covered the phone he was holding, thanked me profusely for my effort, and said he thought mine would probably win. I wondered if he would say exactly the same words to DiMango, to the very inflection, or, being a jazz musician, he'd try to vary his solo.

Outside on the street, the fifth phone I found was the first phone that worked. I called Raymond and told him about McIntyre's gambling debts and lust for Gordell's job. He told me that, to no one's surprise, the bullets dug out of our building wall came from the same gun that killed Dave Krulick. "Also, your man, Big Stan, is in the clear. We weren't sure about his alibi for the night Gordell was killed, but we finally got to the woman he said he was on a date with, and it checked out. On the night Dave Krulick was killed, he was on a session with seven other people, and he's got a used plane ticket that says he was in Syracuse when someone took a shot at you."

"What about the tape?"

"It's in the audio lab. We should know something by tomorrow."

***

That evening, Annie and I donned the headphones again and put it through our own audio lab.

"I think I hear something else," she said, after I don't know how many times. "Listen to the noise just before he says 'big.' It's a sort of reed squeak. Well, I think he's saying a word at the same time. Run it again."

I did, and listened so closely I thought my ear drums would implode. I could barely make out his voice, ever-so-softly in synch with the squeak. "It sounds like he's saying 'a big Stan', " I said.

"Yes," said Annie, "doesn't it?"

"This is nuts. I know I asked him a question and he was answering me. If I could only remember the fucking question. It obviously wasn't 'What's the name of your drug dealer?' I was trying to do three things at once, plugging in, checking out the music, and tuning my bass, and he was heckling me. I tossed off some smartass question and he was answering it. Why can't I remember what I said?"

I took off the headphones and began twisting the cord around my fingers. "I remember every other stupid goddamn thing in the world, like that list of fucking warehouses." I wound the cord tighter. "Someone is trying to kill us, honey. He's trying to kill us because of something I know. Because of something that's inside *me.*"

The headphone cord was starting to turn my fingers purple. I drew it even tighter. "I'm the one who asked Lick that question. And if I could only remember it, we would figure out what his answer was." I gave the cord a good yank. "And it could be the answer to this whole fucking nightmare." My fingers were throbbing. I felt a grim, deranged satisfaction in that. I gave the cord an even stronger tug and the pain shot to the tips of my fingers. They felt like they were going to pop like overcooked sausages.

"Why can't I remember the motherfucking question?"

Annie stared at me in alarm. My eyes must have been the eyes of a madman.

"Why?!!!" I wailed.

Chapter Thirteen

Wired Angel, during the late '60s, was the foremost New York recording studio of its time. Hendrix, the Lovin' Spoonful, Vanilla Fudge and, yes, Generation Gap, among many others, did albums there. It occupied the basement of a townhouse on Waverly Place in Greenwich Village, and it was done up in the style of a subterranean grotto, with lava lamps undulating and soft, blue track lighting set into the recesses of cave-like Styrofoam walls. The sweet scent of cannabis always seemed to be in the air.

Its brand-new midtown incarnation was nothing like this. I stepped out of the elevator on the 15th floor of the Picknitter and Ogrely Building into a gleaming world of polished mahogany and chrome. A receptionist resembling Cheryl Tiegs directed me through a double door with bronze lion's heads for doorknobs into the control room of Studio A.

You could have fit the entire Wired Angel of the '60s into this control room. Seated at the console in a massive swivel chair was a young engineer, surrounded by an array of equally massive chairs containing McIntyre, Samuel, Amos, and Fred, who all looked up at me as I came in.

"Hey there, Freak Flag Flyer," Fred called out. "I was just telling the folks here about your long and storied past, before you sold out and joined the establishment."

Amos looked like he was about to ask for my autograph. "Wow, man, I didn't know you were with Generation Gap. You guys were great. My older brother used to play your albums so much, my parents finally threw them out the window."

"Right on," I said.

"Fred has been showing us some falls sounds," said Samuel, who seemed less concerned about my role in American pop culture. "I think we've settled on one…" He looked sternly over at Amos, who rolled his eyes at the ceiling. "…but it has to be longer than three seconds, or else it sounds like a toilet flushing."

"Longer is fine with me," I said. "And, as a matter of fact, I have a vocal effect in mind that I wanted to show you." I got out the guitar and sang them my idea for the group to sing the word "falls" in cascading layers.

"I don't want to put the sound effect under that," said Amos with concern. "That's the wrong part of the song."

"We don't have to," said Fred. "This is a separate effect."

"Maybe we can put it under your rainbow shot, Amos," said Samuel. "It might help it out."

Amos again rolled his eyes.

"Where's Joel?" I asked.

"He had to beg off to baby-sit a client," Samuel replied. "It's just as well. He was starting to get interested enough to make suggestions."

McIntyre, who, along with DiMango, now shared my focus since Hook's elimination, stared through the glass into the studio. "I think the musicians are here," he said to no one in particular.

And indeed they were. I grabbed the music, excused myself, and went out to run it down for them. The instrumental track presented no problems. After we'd gotten a particularly good one, I went back inside the booth to sing the melody over it for McIntyre, Samuel, and Amos, just to give them the idea. Then we did a couple of guitar and synthesizer overdubs, and that was it for the musicians.

Annie was the first singer to arrive. Fred gave her a hug and then, for Samuel and Amos's benefit, expounded on her hit records with the Love Notes. This time, Samuel was the one who was impressed, actually blushing.

Dawn, Eileen Watkins, DiMango, and Adonic trickled in. I looked for any signs of resentment on DiMango's part, but it was hard to tell. He gave me the same perfunctory greeting as always. I took them all out to the studio to show them the vocal arrangements.

My fears about Adonic as a group singer were well-founded. I sang him his individual part and discovered his amazing superpowers did not extend to harmony.

"This is a bitch, man," he whispered to me as he stared intently and uncomprehendingly at the music. To make matters worse, I'd written some pretty complicated vocal parts that would have been challenging even for experienced group singers.

"Why don't we try this?" I suggested softly. "I'll sing your part with you on the basic track and then switch to my own part on the overdub, while Bobby sings your part with you. Then we'll do a third pass, where Bobby and I will double our own parts and if you still haven't gotten it, no problem. You can mouth it. Is that okay with you, Bobby?"

He glanced self-consciously at Adonic. "Sure, man, just let me study it a minute."

"I could even do it on the third pass," said Annie. "Most of it isn't too low."

"I feel like such a fucking cripple," said Adonic.

"Never you mind, baby," Eileen Watkins said. "My heart's got wheelchair access."

I asked the engineer to play the instrumental track, and we began to work on the blend. "Take one of your headphones off," I advised Adonic, "so you can hear the rest of us."

"Is there a part missing?" asked Fred through the intercom.

"It'll sound that way on the basic," I said carefully, making eye contact with him through the glass. "We'll fill it in on the double."

"Got you," said Fred. "Okay, why don't we try one?".

Forty minutes later, as we filed into the control room to hear the playback, Annie fell into step next to me. "Anything new and exciting?" she whispered.

"Perhaps as we speak," I said, noticing that McIntyre had gotten up from his chair, moved next to Adonic, and was talking to him as the music poured forth from the speakers.

"Time to drop some eaves," said Annie as she moved behind them, pretending to rummage through her purse. Neither of them noticed.

Whatever McIntyre was telling Adonic wasn't making him too happy. I didn't know how much of it Annie could hear because the music was so loud, but, as it ended, McIntyre seemed not to realize it for a second and continued talking. Annie moved away from them, giving me the slightest of nods.

"Can I ask you something?" said Samuel. "How do you pronounce the word 'falls'?"

Everyone laughed, but I didn't. Even though I had no idea where this was going, I knew he was serious.

"Falls," we all said, one at a time.

"That's what I thought," he said. "Here in New York, you pronounce it 'fawls,' but I think the rest of the world pronounces it 'fahls.' Can we listen to it again?"

We did and it still sounded heartland America to me. "There," said Samuel, "can you hear it? It sounds like 'fawls.' Is there any way we can fix it?"

"Sure," said Fred. "We can erase everything and do the whole session over again."

"Would that be a problem?" asked Samuel.

We trooped back out into the studio. "Hey man," Adonic said to me as we made our way toward the microphone, "I think I can sing my part now."

I couldn't help thinking, *Really? Did McIntyre sing it to you just now?* There was definitely some sort of arrangement between them, and it wasn't musical.

"Does anyone have another session they have to get to?" I asked.

"I do," said Dawn, predictably. "But I can make a phone call between takes and I'm sure they'll understand."

"That's more than you can say for me," I muttered as we prepared to start from square one.

We gave it the "fahls" treatment for another forty minutes. At one point, I noticed Joel had arrived and was sitting in the booth next to Samuel and Amos, who were both looking glum. *Serves 'em right*, I thought, *for extending the session.*

We finished the last track and entered the booth to listen. This time, Samuel was pleased. Joel nodded to me with a beatific smile.

"Oh, there's something else," he said brightly. "I spoke to the client this morning and he wanted you to put this line in. I have it somewhere." He fished around in several of his suit pockets. "Here it is. 'We always care for you. We're always there for you.' You need to put that in."

"You mean in the song we just finished recording?" said Fred, the vein beginning to stand out in his neck.

"Yes," said Joel, looking around at us and smiling placidly.

"There's no place to put it," I said, "except over the last two bars of the announcer section in the middle. That would mean you'd have less announcer copy. Is that going to be all right with them?"

"It better be," said McIntyre, to my astonishment. "These people should learn to have their act together so that other people can do their jobs."

My God! Could this be our Melvin McIntyre? Was he actually capable of doing his own job?

"Let me figure out a quick melody for it," I said. "And since it reeks of warmth and sincerity, I think it should be a solo."

"I agree," said Fred. "Dawn, how are you doing for time?"

"Actually, I'm fine. My next session at Magnum Opus is running late."

"Okay," said McIntyre, "everyone else can leave now."

Annie and I gave each other a mutually helpless look as people gathered their things and moved toward the door. "Tell you later," she whispered furtively in my ear as we kissed good-bye.

Stifling my curiosity, I grabbed the guitar and went out into the studio to put myself into insta-compose.

It took me a few minutes to come up with a serviceable melody, which I showed to Dawn. She nailed it on the first take, and we went back into the booth to hear the playback of the whole spot.

It sounded terrific, if I do say so myself. The group had a rock-solid, FDIC-insured quality, and Dawn's solo sparkled.

She and Fred stood behind me as we listened.

"You always do it for me, Dawn," I heard him say as it ended.

"I hope so," she answered softly.

Everyone seemed happy with it. I thanked Dawn for staying late, Dawn thanked Fred, Fred thanked McIntyre, and McIntyre thanked Samuel, Amos, and Joel.

As people were drifting out the door, Fred took me aside. "I'm afraid I have to leave you to handle the mix and Melvin by yourself, if that's okay. Julie's got the flu, so I have to run back to the office and answer the phone in a falsetto voice. Good job, old buddy. Give me a call later."

"You bet," I said. "I want to hear this falsetto voice."

"You won't like it. And I don't look so hot in her dress, either."

He said good-bye to the engineer and McIntyre, and split.

As the mix was being set up, McIntyre motioned me over to a corner of the control room. "Now that everyone's gone, I wanted to talk to you for a minute," he said. "You did a very good job on this account. We've got some important things coming up and I'd like to give you some more work. You'd be interested in that, wouldn't you?"

"Sure I would, and thanks," I said cautiously. "But if it's all right with you, I'd like you to hire me through Fred. I don't want to be considered a jingle house."

His eyes rested on me with something between inscrutability and dullness. I couldn't tell whether he was weighing my words or zoning out.

"Whatever," he finally said, waving a dismissive hand, "but I want Fred to know you're the only reason I'm hiring him. Now, there's something else: I understand you've been talking to Hilda."

How did he know that? The possibility that the outer office was bugged came to mind. I didn't dismiss it.

"I just wanted to tell you," he said, "that the less you talk to Hilda Kravitz, the better. She was a little too attached to Harold, and her perspective is off."

"I see," I said, although I didn't.

"We've got some major campaigns in the pipeline, as I mentioned, and I'd like to include you in them. But you should be careful about who you talk to."

"Uh huh."

He put his hand on my arm, looked me in the eye, and nodded, as if we'd just clinched a deal. "Okay. Now I'm going back upstairs and leaving the mix to you. The studio will send it up to me when it's finished. This all turned out very well, and I'm glad we had this talk." He left without saying good-bye to the engineer.

Since the mix involved several layers of group vocals and would be fairly complicated, and since the original session had taken extra time, I knew I was behind schedule for my next job at Phil and Judy's. I called and left a message with their secretary that I was tied up in a mix at Wired Angel and would be running late.

It was after three when I emerged onto Sixth Avenue, which is Avenue of the Americas to everyone but people who live here, and began looking for a cab. Humanity shouldered its way along in both directions as I stepped off the curb and peered into the brisk traffic. All the cabs seemed to be taken.

I was beginning to wonder if I would be better off wrestling my two instruments onto the subway when I felt a violent shove from behind as a foot clipped the front of my ankles. It sent me stumbling into the traffic, the shift of weight by my instruments yanking me further off balance as I tried to keep my feet, which weren't earning their keep. Suddenly, I was pitching face down toward the asphalt.

I barely broke the fall with my arms, a scintilla of a second before I would've broken it with my nose as a woman screamed. But her scream was only a squeak compared to the frenzied screech of brakes that filled the air in that frozen second.

I looked up from the ground in sheer, brick-shitting terror at the wheels bearing down on me.

Chapter Fourteen

Three inches more and I would've been sporting a tire-tread tattoo on my cerebrum. With the screeching sound still in my ears I gaped at the zig-zag pattern up close and personal. Tearing my eyes off it, I rolled over and looked for my instruments. The bass was between the front wheels of the taxi and the guitar was on the ground to my right. I was amazed to find them unharmed.

I gave a thumbs-up sign to the driver, who was emerging from the cab with a stunned expression on his face, and turned to the crowd standing on the curb, gawking, no one actually offering to help. Couldn't be New Yorkers, I thought, had to be tourists.

"Did anyone see him?" I asked, and got blank stares all around.

"You mean the guy behind you?" said a small woman in a fur coat. "What happened; did he push you?"

"He sure did. What did he look like?"

"I didn't see his face. He was wearing a blue parka and a black ski cap; that's all I noticed. I'm sorry."

"That's okay, thanks," I said.

I nodded my way reassuringly through the crowd, looking for a phone booth and fruitlessly trying to figure out who knew I was here and that I'd be leaving around this time. I'd have to include everyone on the session, plus Phil and Judy. When I finally found a working phone, I called Raymond at the precinct house.

"I'm on Sixth Avenue and 44th," I said, looking around me for any blue parkas and black ski hats. "He was waiting for me as I left a session, and he just now tried to push me in front of a cab."

"You all right?"

"Yeah, I'm fine. A woman got a quick look at him, but all she saw was someone in a blue parka and a black ski cap."

"Not enough. No one noticed anything else about him?"

"No one even noticed that he pushed me."

Raymond sighed. "He's getting cruder. Why do you think that is?"

"Saving money on bullets?" I guessed.

"Try, getting more desperate," he said grimly. "And if he is, then he's getting more dangerous. You might want to reconsider that hotel."

I didn't. He paused, and when I said nothing, he continued.

"Okay, up to you. By the way, it looks like you may be onto something with this Boom Box. There seems to be an amnesia epidemic at both agencies as to who added it to the contract. We'll see what pressure we can bring to bear. Meantime, do any of these names ring a bell?"

He read me a list of the seven names on the leases for the warehouses. I'd never heard of any of them.

"Well, the names on the leases aren't always the names on the incorporation papers. We're looking into them too."

"Maybe you should look into Melvin McIntyre. He took me aside today and warned me about talking to Hilda Kravitz. Even offered me work if I'd stay away from her. He said Hilda was a little too attached to Harold. Is it true McIntyre has big gambling debts?"

There was a pause. Who was I, I realized, to be asking him for police information on a private citizen? Actually, I didn't have much status at all in this. I was only, as sleazy as it sounds, an informant.

"All I can tell you about Mr. McIntyre," he said, "is that we're still checking his alibis for the murder nights and the attempt on you and Annie."

"So I should be careful of him."

"Among others. Oh, and the voice analysis on that tape came back. He's saying, ''cause my man's a big unintelligible.'"

Just like everything else.

***

I found a cab, got into it rather than under it, and gave the driver the address for Best Sellers. As I got out, I checked the street in both directions. Nobody looked threatening or familiar, and I made it up to Phil and Judy's without any further attempts on my life.

They were sitting in the control room, staring through the glass at the empty studio as I arrived. Phil, usually the soul of ebullience, managed a weak nod and an almost perfunctory "Hi, Ernie." Judy did the same.

"You won't believe what just happened," I said. "Somebody tried to kill me. Pushed me in front of a cab."

Phil looked up at me as if from under water. "You're okay though, aren't you?"

"Yeah, a little taken by surprise, but all right." I was more than a little taken by surprise at his reaction.

"Someone pushed you?" said Judy in a faraway voice. It was as if I'd stepped into "The Invasion of the Body Snatchers."

"Yes," I said, looking into her eyes, which seemed almost blank in their distraction.

"This city is crazy," said Phil distantly, and then he changed the subject. "Let me show you what we're reduced to doing."

He picked up a piece of music that had been lying on the console and gave it to me. "This is for a product that doesn't exist yet, and I can't believe it ever will."

Forcing myself to set aside the strangeness of the vibe, I looked down at the music. The tune went:

What's the nicest thing to be next to?
We'll give you a hint
It's the chlorophyl-scented bathroom tissue
Excre-Mint

"And besides that," said Judy, "the agency doesn't even have the account. They're competing for it and there are supposedly three other jingle houses besides us."

"We can only pay you a few bucks for doing the demo," said Phil. "They gave us practically no money."

"That's okay," I said. "You guys have done a lot for me."

"Well, we appreciate it," said Judy, her voice drifting again. "Oh, and by the way, we didn't get Derry Air."

"That's too bad," I said to Phil's back. He'd already gotten up and was heading toward the studio.

"Get Mike in here," he said to Judy over his shoulder, "and we can start running it down."

I followed him out and we recorded the instrumental track in the usual way, with Phil playing piano and me playing guitar on the first pass, then switching to drums and bass. There was no conversation, and he accepted the first take we did on everything. When I asked if he wanted me to do another guitar part, or if he wanted to overdub synthesizer, he dismissed it.

"Nah, this is fine. You and Judy do a couple of group tracks, but don't kill yourselves over it. I have to go out for a while."

He got up and went into the control room. I could see him through the glass, muttering something to Judy before going out the door. After a moment, Judy came out into the studio.

"Is everything okay?" I asked her.

"Let's do this thing first," she said. "If I start talking about it I won't be able to sing."

We did the melody, doubled and tripled it, added a few harmony tracks, and listened to the playback through the studio speakers.

"Sounds fine, Mike," she said. "Why don't you mix it?"

"You want me to mix it myself?" The incredulity in Mike's voice was apparent, even through the intercom.

"Yeah," she said. "I'll check in after a while to see how you're doing, but I'm sure it'll be fine."

"Excuse me," I whispered. "It might be none of my business, but what the fuck is going on?"

"Let's get out of here and get some coffee."

We went downstairs to the coffee shop in the building. It was almost deserted, and we took a booth in the back. The coffee tasted like it had been waiting a long time, and now it was seriously pissed off.

"I don't know what Phil's doing or where he goes. He hardly speaks to me." Judy's voice cracked and her eyes started to fill with tears. She shook her head vehemently, drew in a deep breath, let it out slowly, and continued clear-eyed.

"He goes out and doesn't come back until late at night, giving me lame excuses. Every night last week. I don't know if it's another woman, but I do know our business has dropped off to practically zero. And I feel like he blames me for it."

"Why would he blame you?"

She looked at me as if trying to decide how much to reveal. "You know the story about us, don't you? What happened after we went public?"

"I know you couldn't work for any other jingle houses."

"That part was fine," she said. "We both knew my career would be over, but I let it happen because I loved him. And I've never regretted it a single day." She looked down into her untouched cup of coffee. "What we didn't expect was Phil's business disappearing. And it's all that fucker Harold Gordell's fault, may he rot in Hell."

This was, of course, going to be the story Annie had heard from Dawn.

"I once sang on a demo for one of his wretched shows and the egotistical bastard blamed me when he couldn't get it produced. That's why he made poor Phil suffer. And now, Phil's blaming me for what Harold did. I don't know how else to account for it. Oh shit."

She was starting to cry. I didn't have any tissues, so I gave her my napkin and grabbed a couple of others from an adjacent table.

"Why would he do that, Judy? Especially after all these years?"

"Business has been slow, but never this bad," she said, drying her eyes. "I'm frightened. I know he always hated Harold, and now this bizarre behavior. God, I don't know why I'm telling you this."

"What are you frightened about?"

She covered her face with her hands and slowly shook her head, as the words seemed to tumble out between her fingers.

"I don't know where he was the night Harold was killed. He told the police he was here on a session we were doing. But actually, he left after the instrumental track and didn't come back until the mix. I needed to ask him about something during the vocals and no one could find him."

"Oh, man," I said, thinking also about the "every night last week" part of what she'd said. I realized I had to be careful.

"Let me ask you something. I called earlier today and left a message that I was running late at Wired Angel. Were you here then?"

She lowered her hands from in front of her face and looked at me.

"No. Lois, our receptionist, told me you called, and that Phil was in earlier and she told him too."

"Then, Phil went out again after he picked up the message?"

"That's what she said. What are you getting at?"

"I don't know; strange things have been happening to me lately. When did Phil get back?"

"About five minutes before you came. Why?"

"Was he wearing a blue parka and a black ski cap?"

She stared at me, with as much disbelief as any of those people who'd seen me emerge from under the cab. Then her eyes blazed.

"I don't want to talk about this. I'm sorry to burden you with my problems, Ernie." She fumbled in her purse, slammed down some money on the table, and slid out of the seat.

"I've got to go back upstairs now and check on the fucking mix. Thanks for your help." She practically ran out of the coffee shop.

"That's okay," I whispered in the empty booth. "You guys have done a lot for me."

Chapter Fifteen

I'd left my instruments upstairs in the studio, and I had to get them before I could leave. Fortunately, Judy was not in the control room as I hurriedly gathered them up and snuck out. As the elevator descended streetward, I tried to wrap my mind around the concept of Phil as a cold-blooded killer. Was it really Phil in that car? Good old, amiable Phil?

My head was on a swivel as I walked out onto the street and started looking for an attacker and a cab at the same time, hoping the cab would come first.

Annie was still at a session when I arrived home, and she wouldn't be back for another hour. I secured the three locks to our dark and curtained apartment and switched on the lights. The cats, who checked me out as I came in, liked this new arrangement, since they could see in the dark anyway, and the increased curtain terrain just meant more clawing pleasure. As I was changing their food I considered calling Raymond and telling him what I'd learned about Phil, but it felt so crazy that I wanted to talk to Annie first.

She got home around 7:30.

"I know you're about to tell me what McIntyre said to Adonic," I said as I met her at the door, "but first, we have some breaking news: Judy thinks it's Phil."

She was starting to hang her coat in the closet and it slithered to the floor, completely escaping notice.

"What!?" She looked at me like she did the night before, when I was throttling my fingers.

I told her about my afternoon with Phil and Judy and then mentioned the part about the tire inspection.

"No, no," she said, "this is way too scary." She came into my arms and held on to me. "Maybe we should go back to the hotel."

"Maybe," I said, "but we don't have to decide right now. And since we don't, let's think for a minute about Phil."

She slowly drew away from me and shook her head.

"Hard to imagine it. I can see Judy being worried because he slipped out of their session that night. I can see him hating Harold all these years. Maybe I could even see him killing Harold in a moment of rage, but what's the rest of it all about? Why would he have it in for you?"

I didn't know.

We started toward the kitchen. "While we're thinking about Phil," she said, "we can also think about what McIntyre could've meant by 'paying free.'"

"Paying free? That's what he said to Adonic?"

"As oxymoronic as it seems, that's what it sounded like. And I wasn't about to ask Brad Adonic, when I got to my next job and discovered I was working for him."

I stopped at the kitchen entrance, confusing the cats in the process.

"Your next job was for Brad Adonic?"

"To my great surprise. I'd accepted a record demo booking for some music publishing company…" She noticed the look on my face. "I know, honey, I shouldn't take bookings from people I never heard of because of your Face the Music experience, but this wasn't some dark alley. This was a studio I've worked in. So I figured it was safe, which it was. Safe but strange."

I started to put some coffee on. The cats gave a brief glance at their dishes and looked up at us. Even though I'd put down new food less than an hour before, they didn't want to commit to it in case we had an attack of the stupids and were about change it. When they saw we weren't, they took a few casual bites and sashayed out.

"What was strange about it?" I asked, while all this was going on.

"It was Brad Adonic's song, and he seemed to be running the show, but the whole time we were singing the background vocals he kept conferring with these four guys in suits who were in the booth. He never introduced them to us. From the instrumentation on the track, I'd say this was a very expensive session for a record demo. Horns and strings, and they weren't synthesized, either."

"Who did the arrangement?"

"You got me. It could've been Bobby DiMango. He was there, sitting with the suits, but he hardly said anything."

"I wonder if McIntyre has something to do with it. And I want to tell you about what he said to me after the session, but I just realized I'm starving. You want to order out from Hunan Balcony?"

"Great by me."

We did so and were promised delivery in twenty minutes. I told Annie the story about McIntyre's warning to stay away from Hilda, and filled her in on what Raymond said about the mysterious silence at the two agencies.

As I was wrapping it up, the buzzer sounded. Hunan Balcony, right to the twentieth minute. I hit the button that sprung the front door, opened our apartment door, and looked down the hallway. But it wasn't an Asian face I saw sticking out between the black ski cap and the blue parka of the man advancing toward me. It was Phil Sellers.

I slammed and bolted the door. "Annie," I called into the kitchen where she was putting out the plates. "It's not the food delivery. It's Phil. I'm gonna talk to him through the door. Get near the phone so you can call 911 if you have to."

By this time Phil was ringing the doorbell.

"Hey, Ernie, what's the matter?" he was saying through the door. "Everything all right in there?"

"Everything's fine in here, Phil. What's going on?" Annie had gone over to the kitchen phone and was poised next to it, looking out at me.

"Nothing. Why don't you open the door?"

"Somebody tried to kill me today, Phil. He was wearing a blue parka and a black ski cap, just like you've got on." I peeked through the peep hole and saw a distended image of Phil taking off the cap and looking down at his coat with a puzzled expression.

"Jesus Christ, Ernie, you think I tried to kill you? Why would I do that?"

"I don't know, Phil. Where did you go this afternoon after you got my message?"

"Where I always go. I went back to the Blarney Stone on Eighth Avenue. I've been living there lately. You can call them and they'll tell you I was there. I don't know the number, but you can get it from information. The bartender's name is Eddie; he's my new best friend. I talked his ass off all afternoon."

"Phil, I hope you don't mind if we take you up on it. Annie's got the phone right here."

"Shit, be my guest." Through the hole I watched Phil take a step back to lean against the far wall and go into it harder than intended.

I conveyed the information to Annie who dialed 411, not 911, got the number, and called the Blarney Stone. Eddie confirmed.

I undid the locks and let Phil in.

"Man," he said, unzipping the blue parka that was like a million others in this city, "I've been accused of many things in my twisted life, but never of trying to kill my friend."

"You don't know what we've been going through, Phil," said Annie as she hung up his parka. "Someone shot at us right outside this building on Friday night, and he tried to kill Ernie today."

"Shot at you? My God, I had no idea! I'm so wrapped up in my own problems, I don't notice anything. Here you were, telling me someone pushed you in front of a cab, and I acted like you were telling me it was raining out." Phil's usually ruddy face was florid, his blow-dry hair was more blown than dry, and his shirt flap was flapping over his belt.

"Have you had any dinner?" I asked him. "We just ordered Chinese, and there's gonna be plenty of it. Why don't you join us?"

"No, no. I just wanted to come by because I felt so rotten about how I treated you today."

"Hey, when you're down in the dumps," I said, guiding him toward the kitchen, "you may as well have some dumplings."

The front-door buzzer went off. This time, I looked down the hall and made sure it was the delivery kid before I let him in.

We took the food into the kitchen and set another place. "I should be apologizing to you," I said. "And I should be apologizing big-time to Judy."

"Judy? Why Judy?"

"You mean you haven't talked to her?" I paused as I was about to pour the hot and sour soup from the container to the bowl.

"No, I haven't," he said, idly running his finger along the pattern of his empty plate. "I don't think she wants to talk to me very much."

"I didn't get that impression this afternoon. She was very worried about you."

He smiled, still staring at the pattern on the plate. "Yeah, I guess she'd be worried. She'd be a lot more worried if I told her our rent is going up twenty percent. I've ruined her life, and now I just can't face her." He looked up at us with moist eyes. "But here I go again. Somebody's trying to kill you and all I can do is talk about me."

"You didn't ruin Judy's life, Phil," said Annie. "Why would you think that?"

"I cost her her career."

"That's not what she told me this afternoon," I said. "She told me she's never regretted a single day."

He gave his plate another rueful smile. "That's nice of her to tell you that. I guess sometimes she does feel that way." The smile faded and he looked up. "But not most of the time. You gonna pour that soup?"

We ate. As we did, the talk got around to Annie's session with Adonic. Phil hooted derisively at the mention of his name.

"There's a case for you. All the God-given talent in the world and absolutely no substance. Except for the substance he puts up his nose."

"What do you know about Melvin McIntyre?" I asked.

"You mean the sportsman? The high roller? What a phony! When I used to work for Harold, all Melvin could talk about were these racehorses he owned with some other agency people. His share was probably the part where the horseshit comes out."

"I heard him talking to Adonic today," said Annie, "and he said something that sounded like 'paying free.' Does that mean anything to you?"

"Paying free? That doesn't even make sense. McIntyre said this?"

"That's what it sounded like."

Phil thought a moment. "Could he have said 'Pain Free'? That used to be the name of a pain reliever, until it was pulled off the market. It was a big scandal at Picknitter, and it got Melvin his job."

Annie and I had picked up our fortune cookies and we now stopped in mid-break.

"That might've been it," said Annie. "What scandal?"

Phil idly spun his fortune cookie on the table in front of him. "Frank Fletcher, the guy who used to be Harold's assistant before Melvin, had a brother-in-law who was the CEO of a pharmaceutical company. They made this pain reliever called Pain Free and did their advertising through Picknitter. The feds later discovered that both Fletcher and the brother-in-law were skimming profits and, on top of that, the company was lacing the capsules with codeine so they'd be more effective. The product got pulled and there were all kinds of lawsuits. Picknitter wound up paying a chunk of change, just to relieve their own pain, and Fletcher was relieved of both his job and his freedom. Melvin McIntyre was the beneficiary of it all."

"Why would he be talking about it with Brad Adonic?" Annie wondered.

"Why would he be talking about anything with Brad Adonic?" said Phil. "Where did this happen, on a session?"

"This afternoon," I said. "McIntyre had me use Brad Adonic as a group singer."

This sent Phil into such spasms of laughter, I thought he might be having a stroke.

"Oh, man, that's great!" he guffawed. "Adonic couldn't get arrested up there when Harold was in charge, and now McIntyre's forcing him on jobs as a…as a…group singer?" He was practically falling off the chair.

I was more interested in the first part.

"He could never work for Harold?" I tried to interject while he was wheezing and drying his eyes with his napkin.

"Huh? Oh no, never in a million years. Harold hated him. You know how he felt about rock 'n roll." Phil looked down at his fortune. "'You have a lively interest in music and the arts.' Fuck, this isn't a fortune. The fortune cookie industry is ripping us off."

I finished breaking mine open. "McIntyre's got something going with Bobby DiMango too. He got him in on the competition for the spot. Directly, not through a jingle house."

"No kidding," said Phil. "That's interesting. Now Bobby DiMango, there's another walking chemistry lab."

Annie looked at her little slip of paper. "'Romance is coming.' Well, I always thought it was more than that."

"Did you ever hear the Cojones Beer story?" I asked Phil.

"Sure, Harold screwed him out of it."

"So it's true. He said it wasn't."

"What? Everyone knows he was the one who wrote that tune, and now you say he denied it? That's really odd."

"It makes you wonder," I said to Annie. "All the elements are there, even the drug angle. Why does it have to be the lone gunman theory? Maybe only one of them killed Gordell, but they all could be in on it." My eyes drifted down to the little fortune in my hand. It said, "You will always be safe at home."

The phone rang.

We all jumped. I think Phil did because Annie and I did.

I picked up the receiver. Loud music filled my ear and a voice shouted over it.

"Hey, man, it's Brad Adonic!" I could hear the sound of his hand being placed over the phone and his muffled voice yelling at someone to shut off the music. It stopped and he came back on.

"Hope I'm not disturbing you, man. Your wife was outta sight this afternoon. She sang great; I love her. I hope I'm not disturbing you."

"No, not at all," I said.

"Listen, man, I got a shitload of trouble here. We're trying to mix this song and the bass part really sucks. Can I ask you a favor? What are you doing now?"

"We just finished dinner."

"Man, can you help me out? I really need you. I'll pay you triple scale. Can you come down here now and put a bass part on my record?"

CHAPTER SIXTEEN

I covered the receiver and whispered to Annie who it was and what he wanted.

"You're telling him no, right?" It was as close to adamant as she gets.

"I'm not sure. Let's talk about it." I uncovered the receiver and spoke to Adonic. "Listen, can I call you back in a couple of minutes?"

"Sure, man, absolutely. Let me give you the number." He yelled to someone who was with him, "Hey, what's the number here? What's that? 4537? I can't hear you, man, 4527? Okay. Hey, Ernie, it's 555-4527."

"I'll get right back to you, Brad." I hung up.

Phil's eyes gleamed with excitement. "This is fascinating. You really think Adonic, DiMango, and McIntyre killed Harold?"

"Do I really think?" I said. "An hour ago I thought it was you. That's why I want to do this thing, because I'm tired of not knowing what I really think." I looked pleadingly at Annie. "It'll be okay if we call Raymond first, tell him where I'm going, and put him on the alert."

"Put him on the alert for what? You just assume you can call him if there's trouble. What if you can't?"

"That's why I'll call you after I check out the situation. But only if everything's okay. If you don't hear from me in, say—forty-five minutes after I leave, call the cops."

"If you don't call in, say—forty-five minutes, you could be, say—dead! No, I'm not just sitting here. If you're going, I'm going with you."

"Honey, I know how you feel. But I don't want to worry about them holding you hostage in the control room. I think you should stay here, and be the liaison with Raymond."

"Hey, I want to go," said Phil. "This is exciting."

"The only place you should go," said Annie, "is home to Judy. You've been acting so weird lately, she's worried sick about you. She even told Ernie she thought you might've killed Harold."

"She what!?" Phil jumped up from his chair, knocking a spare rib off his plate onto the floor, where it landed at the feet of an incredulous Pyewacket. "Is everyone nuts? How could she think that?"

"You told the police," I said, stooping down and rescuing the spare rib, "that you were at a session all night the night of the murder, but she went looking for you during the vocals and you were gone."

"Oh shit, I just went to the bar. I didn't want anyone to know, and I thought nobody would miss me."

"Well, they did," I said. "And now Judy doesn't know where you are, and she thinks things are even worse than what you've been afraid to tell her. You should go home to her."

"I never realized."

"Honey," said Annie, "if you're determined to go to this Adonic thing, let Phil come with you at least as far as the door to make sure no one's waiting for you outside."

"Right. Good idea. Okay, time to call Raymond."

I did it the way we had to when he was off duty, through Gelb at the precinct. In a few minutes, Raymond called back. I told him about the possible Adonic-DiMango-McIntyre connection and recounted the phone call from Adonic and my plans to take him up on it.

"Let me ask you something," he said. "Do you really need the money? Why are you doing this?"

It was a good question. "I just want it to end," I said.

I knew it wasn't that simple, that it had something to do with uncontrollable static from my bass amp, and uncontrollable rage against helplessness. But how could I say that?

"Sure, you want it to end," said Raymond, "but the guy just tried to kill you, and now you're charging out there? This wouldn't be about Vietnam, would it?"

He'd totally lost me. "Vietnam?"

"You remember it. Hang a right when you get to Cambodia. You may also remember the first time I interviewed you, I said I didn't much care for people who avoided service back then. Are you trying to prove something to me?"

"I don't think so," I said, mulling it over. "But I've got nothing to prove, in any case. Just like we had nothing to prove over there. The way I feel is, if Adonic is involved in this, we can find out tonight. If he's not, we can eliminate him. Vietnam's got nothing to do with it."

There was silence. Then, "I'm going to give you a number where you can always reach me. I hope I never hear from you on it. Now, what's this studio you're going to?"

I asked Annie for the name.

"Pungent Sound," she said, with more than a soupçon of resignation. "347 West 47th, between Eighth and Ninth."

I passed it along to Raymond, who gave me what I guessed was his home number. I wrote it down, and we hung up.

Then I reached over and drew Annie into my arms.

"Don't worry, honey," I said softly as we held on to each other. "I'll be okay."

"I didn't marry Timothy Leary, I married Charles Bronson."

Still holding her, I picked up the phone and called Adonic.

"Okay, Brad, I'll do it."

"Wow! Awesome, man. This is gonna save my ass! You know where we are?"

"Pungent Sound, right?"

"That's it. Thanks, man. And I'll have something waiting for you when you get here."

I hoped he meant dope, not death. Although he certainly could have meant both.

***

Phil and I quickly caught a cab on West End and, with the sparse weekday evening traffic, were in front of the studio building on 47th within ten minutes. It was a small building with a well-lighted hallway leading to an elevator in the rear, in plain sight of the entrance. Phil kept his plain sight on me until, with a wave, I got into the obviously empty and ambush-free elevator.

The studio was on the fourth floor. I stepped out into a dark reception area, and practically into the arms of a huge biker type who materialized in front of me, black motorcycle jacket, bandanna, leering smile with teeth missing, and all.

I saw this for only a second by the light of the elevator, before it shut its doors behind me, plunging us into darkness.

"You must be the lamb for the slaughter," he said, and giggled.

"I must?"

I fought the urge to lunge back toward the elevator and jab for the button in the darkness, hoping against hope the car was still there.

The biker stepped over to the control room door and pulled it open, revealing further darkness, except for the dim lights from the console.

"Hey, Brad, he's here," he called into the room and stood back, indicating that I should go inside.

I edged past him and entered the smoky booth as my nostrils were greeted by that old familiar scent. Adonic was sprawled in a swivel chair. He looked up at me.

"Hey, all right! My man has arrived!" He sprang out of his sprawl and threw his arms around me in a big bear hug. I could feel my bass pressing into my rib cage.

He's holding me so the Hell's Angels guy can conk me on the head, I thought in panic and began to struggle to break his grip.

Adonic suddenly released me. I lurched against the console, barely keeping my balance.

"The liberator is here!" said a voice in the darkness. Squinting into the corner, I saw Bobby DiMango lying across a plush chair with a small, metal hash pipe in his hand.

"The rescuer has come to save the captive citizens of Soul Land from the tyranny of the evil despot, Vanilla Bass. We will have freedom of funk." He giggled and tried to get out of the chair, succeeding after a couple of attempts.

"Hey, man," said Adonic, "I really appreciate this. I used the bass player from my backup band and he's a motherfucker on stage, but he just doesn't cut it in the studio. Here, check this out."

He reached into his pocket and got out a small envelope, which he opened and gently shook out over a pocket mirror on the console. The cocaine looked orange in the light. A tiny pile accumulated, and he began to chop it and push it into lines with one of the razor blades the engineer uses to splice tape.

"Looks great, Brad," I said, keeping one eye on the biker, who settled into the engineer's chair and began making tiny adjustments on the board. "But why don't you let me get into the tune first?"

"We got grass, we got hash, we got blow," sang out DiMango. "We got all manner of dope for the savior. But I'm afraid we're out of frankincense and myrrh." He giggled again.

"You want me to play it, Brad?" asked the biker.

"Yeah, sure, Dan," Adonic said. "Let my man hear the damage."

The tune came on the speakers. It was a pop-funk romantic ballad, the title of which, as I gathered, was "All Day Sucker But All Night Lover." Adonic's voice was telling some female how, even though he was just an ordinary guy by day, he was an incredible cocksman by night, and, if she gave him the chance, he would take her to worlds undreamed of. One part of the lyrics said, "Lay your head and rest there. Nestled in my chest hair."

I saw what they meant about the bass part. It seemed to plod along without putting out the necessary pop to drive the rhythm section. The best you could say for it was that it was functional. What it needed to be was funktional.

DiMango handed me a sheet of notebook paper with some chord changes written on it. "We didn't have any music for the rhythm section because they were Brad's band and they knew the song, so I wrote this out for you," he explained.

"Okay," I said, looking out into the dark studio. "Does the light on the music stand work?"

"Hey, I hope you're cool with keeping the lights this way," said Adonic. "It really helps the mood."

"Gotta help that mood," I said, picking up my bass and starting to feel my way out of the control room into the studio. Focusing on the bass amp's power light to guide me, I found it and switched on the music stand light. I groped around under the chair until I found a set of headphones.

"Let me know if you need more of anything," Dan said to me over the intercom. "We killed the old bass part."

And soon, you'll kill the new bass player, I thought crazily as the tune began in my phones. They'd wait to get a good performance out of me first, I figured. Unless they didn't like what I was playing.

I let one verse go by, just to hear it, and then jumped in on the repeat. If you ignored the attitude of the lyrics, it was a good tune with a nice groove and some interesting and unexpected chord changes. Despite myself, I began to get into the music.

It moved through the release and back to the original feel, supported, this time, by horn figures punching the off beats and strings floating between them. My bass settled into the pocket with the drummer and became one with the groove. We were into the extended fade-out now, with the figure repeating and repeating hypnotically as a sax solo sailed above it, spinning curlicues of…something was being pressed into my side.

I didn't bother to think. I threw myself off the chair to my left, away from the gun, and pivoted, bringing the butt end of my bass around hard into the face of the figure behind me.

He threw up his hands and staggered backwards, his heel catching the bass amp and sending him reeling into the partition, knocking it down as he fell on top of it. A small object went flying through the air and landed at the foot of the music stand.

Does he still have the gun? I thought frantically. Whatever just fell wasn't big enough to be a gun. I looked down. The music stand had inverted, so its light was now shining on the floor. There, almost framed in the spotlight, was a hash pipe.

"Holy shit, man!" moaned DiMango, trying to pick himself up off the fallen partition. "What the fuck is the matter with you?"

I squinted through the darkness to see if I could spot a gun in his hand, but I was already starting to feel foolish.

Taking off my bass, I went over to help him up. "Man, Bobby, I'm sorry. You shouldn't sneak up on me like that. You scared the shit out of me."

"I was just gonna ask you if you wanted something from the coffee shop." He was stumbling over the partition and leaning against me. It had been hard enough for DiMango to get out of the chair in the control room, let alone this. "Shit, why did you hit me?"

"I'm sorry, man, but to be perfectly honest, I thought you were sticking a gun in my ribs."

DiMango peered at me like I'd lost my mind. His glasses were no longer on his face, having flown off when I hit him with the bass, and there was a small cut on his cheek.

"You thought I had a fucking gun? What are you, some kind of paranoid lunatic?"

Meanwhile, Adonic and biker Dan had come into the studio to see what was going on, which was good, because I wanted them to hear.

"I'm sorry I overreacted, Bobby, I really am. But in the last four days, I've been pushed in front of a cab and shot at. So I've gotten kinda edgy about people coming up on me."

"Really?" said Adonic, wide-eyed. "Shot at?"

"Somebody tried to kill you?" said Dan.

"Really," I said.

Either they were honestly shocked, or were acting their asses off. My feeling was, their asses were on.

"Jesus, how was I supposed to know that?" said DiMango, flexing his jaw. "I was just trying to get your attention."

"Well, you got it," I said. "Why don't we turn on some lights in here and look for your glasses before we step on them? How's your cheek, there?" I looked as closely as I could in the dark. "Doesn't seem too bad. How does it feel?"

"Okay, I guess," said DiMango, touching it with his hand. He laughed. "Fuck, you really got me a good one. I was gonna call out for a burger, and now I hope I can chew it. Like I was saying, do you want something from the coffee shop?"

"No, thanks," I said. "But actually, while we're taking this break, I have to make a phone call."

I asked Dan, who now looked like an ordinary kid in a motorcycle jacket, if he'd turn on the lights in the reception area so I could talk out there. He did so, and Annie answered on the first ring.

"It's okay," I told her. "I don't think they had anything to do with it."

"Are they holding a gun to your head, making you say that? If they are, just say 'uh huh.'"

"No, it's fine," I said softly. "They're just a couple of stoners making a record. I'm gonna hang around for a while after I do the bass part to see if I can find out anything about McIntyre."

"Be careful, honey. I'm not resting easy until you're back inside our locks and curtains."

I went into the studio. DiMango's glasses had been found undamaged, fortunately, so we all settled in. I ran the tune again, and then Dan started taking it. During one pass, I came up with something in the final fade out and chorus that they liked so much, we went back to the first chorus and I replaced what I'd played before. It all took about a half-hour.

They were whooping and clapping each other on the back as I walked into the booth to listen to the final playback.

"Oh baby, did you ever save my fucking ass!" Adonic rhapsodized. "Man, now this motherfucker cooks!" He bent down over the mirror and indulged himself in a long toot.

"Yep, no doubt about it; you are the savior," DiMango wheezed as he attempted to hold in a generous lungful of hash and offered me the pipe. I accepted and took a toke.

"Check out this blow, man," Adonic told me.

"No, that's cool. I'm trying to cut down."

I grabbed a swivel chair and observed them a moment in their binge.

"Who's tryin' to kill you, man?" asked Adonic, through sniffs.

"If I knew that, you could stick me with a hash pipe all you want."

"Does this all have something to do with Harold?" gasped DiMango, tendrils of smoke drifting from his nostrils.

"It would seem to," I said. "And I have to ask you, Bobby, why does everyone say you wrote the Cojones Beer tune?"

"You want to know the truth, man?" He expelled a large cloud and tilted toward me. "I told you I didn't write it because I'm fuckin' sick of people talking about it."

"Bobby sure wrote this tune," Adonic said, looking over at him with love in his eyes.

"It's a really nice tune," I said, "and I like the horns and strings. Is Melvin McIntyre helping you with the finances?"

Adonic gave a short, barking laugh. “He was supposed to, the fucker.” He scraped together another line of coke and snorted it up. “Now he’s tellin’ me I’ve gotta lay out the bread for this session; do you believe it? He says he’ll pay me back next week, after this horse of his runs. Fuckin’ asshole.”

I considered this. “Would the horse’s name happen to be Pain Free?”

Adonic sniffed and rubbed his nose against the back of his hand. “Yeah, but who gives a shit? Hey, Bobby, do you want to mix it tonight? Are you game, dude?”

DiMango wasn’t listening. He was staring straight ahead. “It was bad enough Harold fucked me,” he said. “But what fries me even more is that I have to be nice to all these jingle house assholes, while they laugh at me behind my back for letting Harold screw me. Big fucking joke.”

He shook his head and chuckled bitterly. “But there was someone who was an even bigger idiot than I was, I can tell you that. Whoever the poor sonofabitch was who wrote the Old King Cola jingle for Harold got fucked much worse than I ever did.”

“You mean, the one with people lined up the length of the Grand Canyon and singing?” I asked.

“Fuckin’ A. The one that wound up with a record version that went platinum. Harold got the schmuck who wrote it to sign an agreement relinquishing all rights. Then he froze him out of the spot. All those versions were produced by different jingle houses. This guy not only wasn’t on the contract, he didn’t even get to produce it. Harold paid him a couple of bucks for the tune and that was the last he ever got. Pretty fuckin’ stupid, huh?” He laughed again, beginning to work up a real good time over it.

“Yeah,” he said, “I’d like to know the name of that poor fucker.”

So would I, I thought. *So would I.*

Chapter Seventeen

I was on the phone with Raymond bright and early, filling him in on Adonic and DiMango and reporting the Old King Cola story. And there was one other thing.

"You mentioned Vietnam last night. Do you still feel that way about people who opposed the war?"

"Not like I did then. But I still don't forgive their tactics. You ever recall saying things like 'off the pig'?"

"The closest I ever came to that," I assured him, "was when I ate a ham sandwich."

It got a chuckle. "Glad to hear it. But back to the present, where will you be today?"

"At Magnum Opus 'til around three, then a session with Izzy Shleppman at five." When I'd called the service for messages the night before, to my surprise, there was a Shleppman job waiting. I worked for the guy twice a year, and now I was seeing him twice in two weeks.

"I'll probably be in touch with you," said Raymond. "We may get some of the names behind the names behind the warehouses. And maybe Boom Box too." It sounded good to me.

I looked up and down the street before I stepped out the front door, and continued to behave in that manner until I was inside a cab. Arriving at Magnum Opus without incident, I found George in his office, his desk a sea of papers.

"Well, you're early for a change," he said, smiling up at me. "I'm in the middle of paperwork, but it's good paperwork." His smile broadened. "Are you all set to meet our Minnie Sweet? She's my favorite client."

"Any favorite client of yours, et cetera," I said. "I wanted to ask you something."

"Yes?"

"Do you remember the Old King Cola jingle of a few years ago? The one with the Grand Canyon?"

"My granddaughter still performs it with her school chorus."

"Have you ever heard anything about Harold Gordell buying the rights and screwing the writer?"

George looked at me for a long moment. "I don't think anyone knew who the writer was. There were rumors at the time that Harold pulled a fast one on him, but since no one ever complained, I always wondered if he had." He clasped his large hands over his ample abdomen and slowly twiddled his thumbs. "But then again, I can understand not wanting people to know you were taken by Harold. It's not good to look bad in this business." He glanced over at the clock on his desk. "Well, to work we go."

I followed him across the reception area, about to meet the reason for his unusually upbeat manner. She was just stepping out of the elevator, a tall, elegant woman in her fifties in a sable coat, with long, dark hair pinned high atop her head and absolutely perfect makeup. She and George spotted each other.

"George, you old dear. How have you been keeping yourself? I can't wait to hear what you have to show me."

"Ah, Minnie," he said, sounding a bit like W.C. Fields, "it's so good to see your beautiful countenance. Allow me to introduce you to the brilliant writer of this piece, Ernie Lanier." Brilliant? I'd never seen George like this. "Ernie, Minnie Sweet."

"Pleased to meet you," she said, delicately taking my hand.

"Likewise," I said. "And I'm only brilliant when I'm lit."

She laughed with almost Dawn-like melodiousness. George took her coat and we all repaired to the control room, where I got out my guitar.

"Now, I must tell you," I warned her, "this has to be pronounced very carefully when we record it. Otherwise it'll sound like 'you reek of cologne.'"

"My goodness," she said. "We don't want that, do we?"

"Usually not," I replied, and sang the tune for her.

Eureka Cologne, that's what they say
Eureka Cologne, by night and by day
The scent of it clings to you, won't go away
With you to stay
Forever, Eureka Cologne

"Oh, it's wonderful," she said.

The musicians showed up and I went out to the studio. Robbie got the proper sound levels, and we did the instrumental track. Minnie Sweet sat in the control booth next to George and seemed to be having a great old time. After a particularly good take, I went into the booth and sang it for her against the track.

"It's even more wonderful," she said.

"And no reflection on Ernie," said George, "but wait 'til you hear Eileen Watkins, our singer, do it."

"I can hardly," said Minnie Sweet.

George escorted her to the clients' lounge while we did some guitar and synthesizer overdubs and, before long, the musicians were finished and Eileen arrived.

"Mornin', baby," she said, sweeping into the control room. "I wanted to tell you yesterday, I just lo…o...oved singing that Niagara Falls tune of yours. Even more the second time." She gave me a mischievous little smile.

"Annie keeps telling me how much she loves the second time," I said.

"Watch your mouth, honey. I'm not used to hearing about such things. You better just show me the tune before I get too excited."

I had Robbie play the instrumental track, and I sang it for her.

"I guess there ain't no way I can avoid gettin' excited." She winked at me as she took the music from my hand.

George and Minnie Sweet came in, introductions were made, and Eileen went out to the studio for the solo.

Midway through, she sang a wrong word and we stopped it. But it sounded so good up to there that we decided to keep what we had and punch in at that spot.

Robbie rolled back the tape and, at the punch-in point, hit the record button. Eileen started to sing, but we didn't hear her. What we heard was the mistake.

"Huh, it didn't record," said Robbie. "This thing has been temperamental lately. Sorry, can we do it again?"

This time it worked. Eileen finished up amid much oohing and aahing by Minnie Sweet and beaming by George.

I went out to the studio to run down the vocal parts with her so that we could be the backup group. If it went final, we'd add other singers but, for the demo, she and I would do all the parts.

As we were doubling the first part, the punch-in mechanism screwed up again. This time it took several tries. Finally, after it failed again, Robbie's voice came over the intercom.

"Listen, I hate to be a drag, but I need to replace this thing. Would you mind taking a twenty-minute break or so? I'm sorry."

We assured him it was fine. George shepherded Minnie Sweet into the lounge, and Eileen and I pulled up two folding chairs and sat down.

"You remember the Old King Cola jingle from a couple of years ago?" I asked her.

"You mean the one they made into a miniseries?"

"That's it. Did you ever hear anything about who wrote it and whether Harold Gordell took advantage of him when he bought the rights to it?"

"You know, I got to sing on a Black version of it when I first started in the business. But I'm afraid the original was before my time, honey. You might ask one of the older singers."

"And you never heard anything about Gordell freezing out the writer?"

"Honey, I just sing the notes and let the screwers screw the screwees all they want. You gotta stay out of the way in this business."

"I'm trying."

We talked about the latest movies and other nonrelated things. Robbie finally came on the intercom to announce man's triumph over machine, and we resumed.

Six tracks of group vocals later, we entered the booth to the accompaniment of applause from George and Minnie Sweet.

"Could I ask a favor of you, Eileen?" she said, showing her a piece of paper with some advertising copy on it. "This is supposed to be spoken over the instrumental section. Would you read it for this demo, just to give the client the idea? If they like you enough, maybe you'll do it on the final."

Eileen looked it over. "Guess you want a sexy voice for this," she said doubtfully. "Sexy voices ain't exactly my specialty."

"That's okay; it's just to give them the idea."

Eileen shrugged. "Well, like I always say, if you can't give 'em sex, give 'em the idea."

She headed out to the studio. Robbie quickly got a level, ran the tape to that point, and she read the copy.

"Hey there, what are you doing? You're driving me crazy with that masculine aroma. Don't you know I'm smelling it with my heart?…" and so on for the allotted twelve seconds. She was right. It didn't sound sexy at all.

"That's just fine," said Minnie Sweet reassuringly.

Eileen returned to the booth, and mutual thank-you's were exchanged all around. As she was leaving, George took me aside.

"We're having time problems since this session took so long. There's another one due in here in fifteen minutes. Now, Minnie has agreed to wait 'til tomorrow morning. Do you think you could come back after seven tonight to mix it with Robbie?"

"Sure. All I've got to do later is play bass for Izzy Shleppman this afternoon, and that'll certainly be over by then."

"Izzy Shleppman, now there's a guy who's been around," said George. "You know, we were talking about Harold before, and Old King Cola. One person who really got the short end of it from Harold was Izzy Shleppman."

"That so? I know Izzy told me he was Harold's pianist when he was trying to get his shows produced."

"That's right, for a long time. Izzy got into advertising before Harold did. In fact, he gave Harold his first contacts. He wouldn't have been in the business at all if it wasn't for Izzy, but you know how much work Izzy got out of it? Zero, as far as I know. A man would feel some resentment about that, wouldn't you think?"

"I'd think," I said.

I shouldered my instrument bags, said good-bye to Minnie Sweet, headed out to the front desk, and asked Tracy if there were any messages for me. There was one, from Raymond.

I told her I needed an outside line, picked up the phone and heard George's voice.

"…I don't know when I'll be getting out of here," he was saying to someone, "so why don't you…"

"This line isn't free," I said, covering the receiver.

"Oh, gosh," she gasped, and blushed. "I've been doing that all week. Try it now."

I did and it worked.

"Good news, bad news about Mr. McIntyre," Raymond informed me. "The good news, for him, is that his alibis checked out. You want to know the bad news?"

"Bad news for me or for him?"

"Only him. We got word just after I talked to you this morning that they found his body in the trunk of an abandoned car in Rockaway."

My instruments slipped to the floor, and I leaned against the desk. "This just keeps going on, doesn't it," I said. "What do you think it means?"

"I don't think it's related. Mr. McIntyre had a gambling jones the size of Vegas. And he made the mistake of borrowing a lot of money from guys who don't let you declare Chapter 11. It all smells like mob. Whatever he had going in the jingle business seems to be beside the point in this one."

"Well, down goes one, up pops another," I said, lowering my voice and carrying the phone away from Tracy's desk. "I just learned something about Izzy Shleppman, the guy I'm going to see next. He got Gordell started in the business and Harold never gave him any work in return. You should see this guy. He does jingles for shoeshine stands."

"Maybe they're all in on it," said Raymond.

"You're kidding, right?"

"You have to ask? Do I detect a desensitization of the sense of humor?"

"You're the detective," I said. "Listen, I've got some time to kill. Maybe I should go up to Picknitter and Ogrely and see what's going on there in the wake of this tragedy. They do know about it, don't they?"

"Oh, they know. They've been duly informed."

"Well, I'll duly inform you if I find out anything. This is getting so weird, I wouldn't be surprised if Hilda is the new music director."

Chapter Eighteen

I left a message on the service for Margie Burnett to call me after five at the Shleppman session. Leaving Magnum Opus, I employed my usual watchful routine and cabbed it to Picknitter and Ogrely.

Hilda was alone in the outer office, talking on the phone in a droning voice, saying McIntyre wouldn't be in today, while her extension lights glowed.

She hung up and looked at me. "I gave my notice. I don't care who they put in here; I'm out of here. Now somebody's killed Melvin."

"What!?" I said in ungenuine shock. "When did this happen? I can't believe it!" I didn't like doing it, but it made things simpler if she didn't know I knew.

"They found his body this morning." She looked down at the winking lights on the phone and started to cry. "Oh, screw all these people. I'm on a break." She wiped her face with a tissue, daintily blew her nose, and then got up and walked over to the coffee maker.

"Do you want some coffee? Let's sit over there in the lounge area."

I parked my instruments against her desk and settled on one of the couches, as she brought over two cups and sat down with me.

"Where is everybody?" I asked.

"They're all at a meeting trying to decide what their official attitude is gonna be when the story gets out. This is a bad place. Things used to be so different. God, I miss Harold. He was such a wonderful man."

"You must have cared for him a lot," I said.

"Nobody knew the real Harold." She looked at me with melting eyes. "He was my best friend. People in this business were only interested in the money he could make them. They didn't care about how sensitive and talented he was." She stared away from me and into space. "And he was so lonely. Nobody ever knew Harold the way I knew him. Not his bitch of a wife, nobody."

Hilda had been a little too attached to Harold, McIntyre had said. I looked into her eyes, which were like pools of tears, and decided to take the plunge.

"You loved him."

She looked back at me with that beautiful, heart-shaped face that was even more beautiful, now that some of the makeup was gone. She reached up and nervously tugged on one of her bangs.

"Yes, I loved him. He was the kindest, most understanding man I ever met. And he loved me too." A tear made its way slowly down her cheek. "There's a beautiful suite of rooms the agency has at the Midtown Plaza for its out-of-town clients. We used to sneak away sometimes and meet there." Her lips trembled as her voice started to break. "He told me we wouldn't have to keep it a secret anymore, that his horrible shrew of a wife was finally going to give him the divorce. It was going to be the last time we'd ever have to meet that way."

She choked back a sob. "And it really was the last time. Because that night someone killed my poor Harold. Oh, God!" She put her head in her hands and wept.

For the second time in less than 24 hours I was absorbency challenged, but I spotted the box of tissues on her desk. I grabbed a fistful, which she gratefully accepted. She was just beginning to dry her eyes when she stopped.

"You know? I wonder if seeing Dawn and that guy had anything to do it."

My heart leaped from andante to allegro. "You saw Dawn Mitchell with a man, at the hotel?"

"Yes," she said, her voice becoming a whisper. "We'd just left our room and I was walking down the corridor with Harold behind me. You had to round a corner before you got to the elevators, and when I did, I could see down to the end of the hallway. And there was Dawn, with some guy, just leaving a room."

"Did you see what he looked like?"

"I didn't have the chance. At first, I was so surprised, I was trying to make sure it was really Dawn. Then Harold pulled me back around the corner."

"Did Harold see them?"

"Yes, that's why he pulled me back before they could turn around and spot us. We waited, 'til we heard the elevator come and go, and then we peeked around the corner again to make sure they were gone. It's funny how I forgot about it. Do you think it's important?"

I remembered something Annie had told me, something Dawn had said…or almost said. Hilda was staring at me, waiting for me to respond.

"I don't know," I lied. "If they didn't see you and Harold, then it wouldn't have mattered. I guess it's interesting as far as Dawn's concerned, but I think that's as far as it goes."

"I suppose," she sighed. "But it was certainly a strange moment. You're so good to listen to me unburdening myself, Ernie. I haven't told anyone about this since it happened, and I don't know why I bothered you with it, but you're one of the few nice people I get to see around here."

I said I felt the same way about her, and that I was honored she would confide in me. Then I looked at my watch, pretended I was late for my next job, grabbed my instruments, and excused myself out of there.

When I reached the lobby, I dove into the first available phone booth and called Annie at our apartment. This was a rare day in which she had no jobs, and we were supposed to have a medium-rare home cooked dinner. So, unless she was out shopping, she should've been home, and she was.

"Honey, do you remember that slip of the tongue Dawn had when she told you about her affair, when she said she was scared about her career?"

"Yes?"

"I think she meant it. I think she's having an affair with someone in the business. Hilda Kravitz just told me that Gordell, on the day he was killed, saw Dawn with her boyfriend."

I could hear her sharp intake of breath. "Oh, man!"

"Oh, man! is right. We all know what happened to Phil and Judy, with a little help from their friend. Tony Trapani said Krulick's dealer is someone in the business; what if he's Dawn's boyfriend? What if he went up there to deliver some coke and Gordell tried to blackmail him?"

"I just thought of something," said Annie. "After we had dinner with her, Dawn, of course, must've met up with him just like she did on the other nights Gerard was working late…"

"She didn't even have to lie about watching 'Dallas.' They could've been screwing during the commercials."

"…and since Dawn loves to go on and on about what she's been doing, she probably told him she just came from dinner with us. She could've even told him we asked her to see 'The Deer Hunter.' She had to get home before Gerard, so they must've wrapped it up well before we got out of the movie. He had plenty of time to come over here and wait for us."

"And how about this?" I said, my adrenaline easing into overdrive. "Raymond said he was escalating things because I must know something. All this time, we thought it was what Dave Krulick said to me, but think back. What was it we were talking about with Dawn in the restaurant?"

"Boom Box," said Annie. "Oh my God."

"Call Raymond, honey, and tell him about this. I have to get downtown to Izzy Shleppman's session. I'll call you from there."

"I should call Dawn too. She could be in danger."

"She could also be in on it. At this point we can't trust anyone."

Annie hesitated. "All right, I guess. I suppose we shouldn't take any chances."

"We shouldn't. We definitely shouldn't. I love you honey; I'll talk to you in a little while. Call Raymond."

***

As the cab made slow but steady progress down Seventh Avenue, I thought about Shleppman's reasons for hating Gordell and I tried to imagine him as Dawn's boyfriend. It wasn't completely impossible. On a scale of physical attractiveness, he was about even with Gerard. Maybe Dawn liked middle-aged men. We pulled up in front of Sound Judgment Studios a few minutes before five.

As I walked in I could hear Izzy talking angrily from Mersh Hamish's office. "Mersh, all I gotta say is I never would've expected it from you. You hear me? Veyge haggit!" He came out of the room and saw me. "You know what that means, boychick? It's Yiddish for go fuck yourself."

"Izzy, is everything all right?"

"Yeah," he said bitterly, "everything is hunky dory. Let me tell you what that bastard is doing to me." He pulled me over into a corner of the reception area. "All of a sudden I've gotta pay him what I owe him. Like I haven't been doing it all these years, that cocksucker, that putz! Now, when I can least afford it, he needs to get paid." He looked at the floor in such a way that, for a moment, I thought he was going to spit on it. "I'm gonna have to find a new place to record."

"You heard about Dave Krulick," I said.

"What?" he said, tearing his attention away from the floor. He actually had to think to remember. "Oh, yes. There's too much crime. Too much violence." He shook his head and looked at the clock on the wall. "Well, if this is my last session in this place, we may as well get it over with."

He walked ahead of me as I tried to figure out his non-reaction to Krulick. Was he so self-absorbed that he honestly forgot? As we entered the studio, I almost crashed into him as he stopped in front of me.

"Look at this bullshit. Do they have to do this during time I'm paying for?"

He was referring to the piano tuner, who was just finishing up, as an engineer's assistant waited to put back the padding that covers the piano. In concert halls, pianos are open, so that the sound can carry. In studios they throw blankets over them, the same ones moving men use to wrap up your furniture. The blankets help contain the sound for the microphones positioned inside.

The tuner packed up, and the engineer's assistant replaced the microphones and draped the padding over the piano under Izzy's baleful glare. Finally all was in place and Izzy introduced me to the guitarist and drummer, whom I'd seen around but hadn't actually worked with before. We all gathered at the freshly tuned eighty-eights, and he sang for us:

Klutzinger's Fabulous Auto Exchange
We've got the name near and far
Cash or on credit
You want it? You'll get it
We'll put you right in that car

There was something familiar about the rhythm of the lyrics, and, as he went into the instrumental music that would be under the announcer, it nagged at me. He made a change of key and began the repeat, and that's when I realized. The lyrics scanned exactly like my stupid warehouse lyrics. You could substitute them for his, and they would fit the music exactly.

National, Corrigan, Belvedere, Blank
Pelican, Global and Spar
Just as you reckoned

It's West Fifty-second
That is the street where we are

For the next hour or so, my mind was everywhere but on what I was doing. I wondered if Margie Burnett had called and left a number where she could be reached. I wondered if it was a total waste of time to suspect Shleppman, even though he was behaving oddly.

I blew a chord change because I played through a repeat sign. This wasn't good. Now it was starting to affect my work. I homed in on the music in front of me, after apologizing for my gaffe. The mood of the tune was very much like the last Shleppman jingle, a thought that brought Dave Krulick to mind with such force that I almost imagined him across the partition from me, just out of sight.

I pulled my attention back to the music. *I wouldn't put my warehouse lyrics to this tune*, I thought. *Too military*. We got a good take at last and heard it back over the studio speakers. Izzy indicated his approval with a wave of his hand, saying, "Okay, we played it. You can go home now. Thanks a lot." He got up from the piano and headed into the booth.

As I was packing up, I was aware of the flurry of activity all around me. Two engineer's assistants were moving the partitions away and setting up the microphones for the vocal session in double time. I assumed it was because Mersh Hamish wanted Izzy out of there as soon as he could get him out.

One of the engineer's assistants slipped in behind me and began to unplug the amp as I picked up my instruments and started across the studio. I was half-way when he called after me.

"Hey, Ernie, I forgot to tell you. You got a phone call from Margie Burnett. She left a number with the receptionist."

"Great," I said, looking back over my shoulder at him.

Suddenly, lightning flashed behind my eyeballs as the side of my head erupted in blinding pain. I staggered and began to fall, my instruments flying out from me. One of the engineer's assistants tried to catch me but couldn't, as I hit the floor on my back.

I lay there dazed, wondering what had just happened. Had I been shot?

"Oh, man, are you all right?" said the engineer's assistant. "You just walked into that boom."

My head throbbed as the word "boom" reverberated through it. Boom—Boom—I walked into a boom. Boom isn't just a sound, it's also a kind of pole.

"As a lyricist," I remembered once hearing, "you should be into all the different meanings of words." A boom is a pole.

And like a tape loop in the background, the warehouse lyrics spun in my brain: National, Corrigan, Belvedere, Blank. Pelican, Global and Spar. A boom is a pole. And so is…

I probably took five years off the life of the engineer's assistant, who was leaning over to gently help me up as I propelled myself off the floor right into him, yelling, "Holy Shit! Holy Shit!!"

Chapter Nineteen

I stumbled out to the receptionist and got the number Margie Burnett had left. Deciding not to use the phone right there, I opted for the privacy of the booth in the outer corridor.

It was evidently Margie's home number. Her answering machine picked up and my heart sank. As I started to leave a message for her, she came on.

"Hi, Ernie. I'm sorry I didn't pick up the phone right away. I'm ashamed to say I'm one of those people who monitor their answering machines. How are you doing?"

"Fine, Margie. I wondered if you could help me with something..."

"Of course, anything. I'm still so embarrassed over what I did. I can't tell you..."

"That's okay, Margie," I hastened to assure and interrupt her. "This isn't about that, it's about something from way back in the past. Do you remember the Old King Cola jingle?"

"You mean the one that became a movie?"

"That's it. Do you know who wrote it? It's really important."

There was a pause at the other end. "Gee, I haven't thought about that in years. And I feel funny talking about it, but I suppose I really owe you guys..." Another pause. "I sang on some of the early versions and tried to keep a low profile because I was on the original piano demo that was presented to Harold..."

I waited for her to go on through silence.

"It was a long time ago, and now Harold's gone, so maybe it doesn't matter anymore. I hope it doesn't..."

I was stretched through yet another excruciating interlude, before she sighed, said, "What the hell," and told me the name I expected to hear, although I still couldn't believe it.

"Thanks, Margie, you don't know what a help you've been."

"Well, you know I'm always glad to do anything. I'm still waiting to get that session check and then I'm going to pay Annie."

"That's great, Margie. Thanks again."

I hung up and dialed our number, setting a new land-speed record for the event. Annie picked up on the second ring.

"I know who it is," I said. "It's Fred."

A pause. I seemed to be creating a lot of pauses.

"Fred? I don't understand. Fred is a wonderful guy who gave us our start in the business. You love Fred. Fred?"

"Boom Box is a cryptic puzzle clue for Spar. Spar Industries is one of the warehouses on Raymond's list. I had to run into a fucking boom stand on the session to realize that a "boom" is a "spar" and "to spar" means "to box." Both "boom" and "box" also mean "spar." It's just like the cryptic puzzles Fred's always trying to get me interested in. He's the only one I know in the business who's into cryptics. Most of the others can't even spell it."

"He does carry around that book of puzzles. But still…Fred?"

"There's more. I just spoke to Margie Burnett. She sang on the original Old King Cola demo. Guess who wrote it? Do you realize how many millions Fred got screwed out of?" Now that I'd started I couldn't stop, as more and more things piled on top of each other.

"When I told him about the argument I had with Gordell, you'd think he would've been at least a little upset, but he wasn't. I know Fred's always on an even keel, but this keel was so even you could balance an egg on it. That's because he knew it didn't matter. We were getting this job from Harold because Fred was supplying him with cocaine, so my little moment of infamy the day before didn't mean anything. He must've hated Gordell, and why wouldn't he? Here we were thinking about Phil and Judy, but look at Fred. People like Stan Hook are building themselves glitzy studios. He's got a two-room office and Julie."

"It's true," said Annie, slowly. "I don't think he works very much, other than what we do with him. But selling drugs? I don't know."

"Why not? He's always going around to the agencies, shmoozing with people. If business is so bad for him, selling drugs would be a great way to improve it."

I imagined what could've happened. "So let's say he's up in Harold's office last Monday night. In a way, it must've been humiliating for him. After all this time, he has to be Harold's drug dealer to get work. Harold, in his avidly avaricious way, tells him he knows about Dawn and tries to blackmail him. It's the straw that breaks the camel hair coat. Fred kills him and then decides he can pin it on me, knowing I'd had a fight with Harold that day and knowing I was home alone working on the jingle. God, I even told him I'd be turning off the phone."

"But can you picture him as Dawn's boyfriend? I'm still trying to get used to this."

I remembered that moment between them in the control room. "You always do it for me, Dawn," he'd said, and she'd answered, "I hope so."

"Fred's a good looking guy, in case you hadn't noticed. He's got a lot of Paul Newman in him. I don't know about Dawn's tastes, but Gerard's much older than she is, and if you're gonna be attracted to older men, you could do a lot worse than Fred."

"You know, now that you got me thinking," she said, "we've never been to his home, we've never even met him somewhere for dinner. Of all our friends, he's someone we never seem to socialize with, maybe because he's a bachelor. We only see him when we're working with him, and aside from how bright and charming he is, what do we really know about him?"

"Not a lot," I said, realizing that we were in a business where how you are is less important than how you present yourself.

Sometimes, what seems bright and charming is just another version of slick and ruthless. I tried to imagine Fred with a gun in that car, and suddenly it wasn't that much of a stretch.

"Honey," I said, "I'm going to call Raymond and tell him about this. Once they know who they're looking for, it won't take long. At least I hope not. You stay right where you are, keep those locks locked, and don't go near the windows. I forgot to tell you before, but I'll be home later than I thought. I have to go back to Magnum Opus and mix that demo. Is it going to louse up our plans for dinner?"

"Dinner will be fine. The steaks can marinate and I'll just quietly stew in my own juices."

"Save some of them for me."

"That's for dessert. And I hope you'll forgive me, honey, but I had to call Dawn. I just can't help feeling that she doesn't know anything about it. I really believe she's being taken in by this guy…Fred…. Anyway, I left word with the service for her to call me and I'm still waiting for her to call back."

"I hope you're right," I told her. What was it Dawn said in the restaurant that night, before her boyfriend tried to kill us? *Maybe I'm a femme fatale.* "Just be careful when you talk to her. I'm going to call Raymond and get over to Magnum Opus. I love you, Annie."

"I love you too," she whispered.

I reached into my pocket for another coin and called Raymond.

"Good timing," he said. "Tell me if you recognize any of these." He proceeded to read off five names that meant nothing to me.

"Are any of them Boom Box or Spar Industries?" I asked.

"No, but we're getting them in a few hours. Why?"

"Because Spar is the one that'll match up," I said, and explained all about cryptic clues. How "a safe leap" was "vault" and "gateway to charm" was "entrance" (and there was something else, but I couldn't think of it), and how "boom box" was "spar" in the same way. I told him Fred was the only one I knew who did cryptics, and that it was he who wrote Old King Cola and got screwed out of millions by Gordell. And how Fred knew I had no alibi for the night of the murder.

"His alibi wasn't too strong itself, as I recall," said Raymond. "He said he talked to you on the phone and went to bed early. You know, of course, what you're telling me isn't evidence. But what we can do is pick up Mr. Allenson for questioning, and if Boom Box and Spar check out to him, like you think they will, we can keep him a little longer. My guess is, once we've searched that warehouse, we can keep him for good. Now where are you? Are you home?"

"I'm about to leave for a mix and then I'm going home."

"You do that. I trust you're being careful. Just be careful a little bit longer and maybe this thing will be over with."

"From your lips to God's handcuffs," I said.

***

I looked up and down the street and all around me for any sign of Fred as I tried to get a cab. I'd never seen him wear a blue parka and a black ski cap, but that meant nothing. I didn't know what kind of coat he was wearing the day before at Wired Angel, since he was there when I arrived and left before I did. The last I'd seen of him was in the control room and all the coats were in the closet outside.

Presently, a cab came and we made our way uptown to Magnum Opus, arriving there a little after seven. I got out of the elevator and walked through the deserted reception area, heading for the main studio. The studio itself was dark, but the control room was well lit and Robbie was there, yanking cables out of the patch bay and replacing them with the configuration of wires necessary for our mix. The sound of a lonely snare drum percussed from the speakers.

"Is George still here?" I asked him.

"Nobody's still here, only the two of us," said Robbie. "We just finished up another mix and everybody took off, so we've got the place to ourselves." He gave me a cockeyed grin and pulled out another bunch of wires.

If you enjoy listening to isolated drum hits, over and over, then the opening phase of a mix is the thing for you. As for me, I would prefer to go somewhere else for a while and watch grass grow. Usually, it takes a bit of time for the engineer to move on to bringing in the rest of the drum set, bass, and the other instruments. That's when I like to come into a mix, so I had a little time to kill.

I walked back into the reception area and started reading a copy of *Downbeat* that was lying on the coffee table, but I couldn't concentrate, so I began wandering around, through the clients' lounge and down the hallway leading to the offices, lost in my thoughts. One of those was that I should check in with Annie to make sure she was all right, and to see if Dawn had called back yet.

A nearby office door was open. I stepped inside and picked up the phone, amidst the clutter of the desk. Midway through our number, a partial word on a magazine cover sticking out from beneath a pile of papers, caught my eye.

"*...PTICS,*" it said.

I moved the papers aside. The magazine cover said *EVERYONE'S FAVORITE CRYPTICS.*

Whose office is this? I wondered as I looked around the room, my blood pressure starting to elevate. On one of the shelves, the smiling face of Dave Krulick looked down at me from an album cover. Hanging up the phone, I went over to it.

All of Lick's other albums were there, lined up behind it. His voice came back to me from behind the studio partition and across the Great Divide. "I've got a new man and he's put me on the Grade A list."

Magically, there it was, that elusive smartass question that had plagued me. "And why would your nostrils be such membranes in good standing?" I'd asked him.

Krulick's answer was as clear as a bell. "'Cause my man's a big fan."

I looked back at the cryptic puzzle magazine and realized that Fred wasn't the only one who made puns, or tried to.

So it should be a nice meeting. And it was nice meeting you. And, *I'd love to stay and hear it, but I've got to dash off. Reps are dashing young men, you know.*

I grabbed for the phone so hard it flew out of its cradle. It went skittering off the end of the desk and hung down the side, making me have to reach across to reel it in. As I feverishly stabbed at the buttons, dialing Raymond's number, I felt a presence in the doorway.

"I'd put down the phone if I were you," said Todd Winston as he leveled a gun at my stomach.

Chapter Twenty

"I don't suppose you're into hot dog skiing."

Winston trained the gun on my midsection as we stood in the control room, where he'd marched me. "No, you could never be one of my ski buddies. The only time you push the edge of the envelope is when you open one of your checks."

Robbie sat in his swivel chair, trussed to it by several layers of duct tape, one strip covering his mouth. Winston regarded me with a sort of dead detachment. The high-cheekboned, Nordic wholesomeness he'd displayed the times I'd seen him before had turned gaunt and angular. His "glad to see ya" eyes were an icy grey.

"I've got a plane to catch in a while, and by the time I get on it, I'll be a whole new man."

Maybe he'll explain to me why he didn't kill me back there in the office, I thought. *Or why he wants to kill me at all. Or maybe he won't explain anything and he'll just kill me.*

I watched, as he placed the gun against Robbie's head, never taking his eyes off my face. Robbie squirmed and made a muffled whimpering noise.

"I'm sorry to have to make you a part of this, Robbie," Winston said, "but you can blame him for that." He pointed it at me again.

"The cops picked you up, I know they did. I saw the police car turning the corner, so what happened? How'd you manage to come back and keep fucking with me?"

Okay, a question means he's interested in the answer. That's why I'm still here. If I can keep him interested, maybe I can keep living. And if I can keep living, maybe I can think of a way not to die.

"I understand why you killed Gordell and Dave Krulick," I said, trying to buy every second I could. "But the cops already know about Boom Box, and killing me doesn't do you any good." I held his gaze and tried to keep my voice even. "I'll tell you what happened with the cops, but first, let me tell you what I think happened with you. You can see if I'm right, okay?" I'd always been told, nothing holds a client's interest more than hearing about himself.

Winston regarded me like a teacher sizing up a wise-ass kid.

"Sure," he said amiably, "why not?"

He pulled Robbie, in his chair, away from the console and faced him toward me. "You can watch too," he said and then looked over at me and smiled. "Go ahead. Tell me about me."

"Well, for one thing, the first time you ever met me was the day after you killed Harold, but you'd already been setting me up. In fact, you'd just come from my apartment."

The smile broadened. Try to make the client's product look good to him. "But of course, you already knew who I was," I told him.

How much time did I have? If Annie heard from Dawn, then she'd know it was Winston, and she'd have called Raymond by now. But not if Dawn was part of it. And maybe she was, I thought, as I realized how he must have known when I'd be leaving Wired Angel. Dawn's next session, as she'd told us, was at Magnum Opus.

"You knew who I was because George told you about me the day before. He said I was going to write the tune for your Burger Meister demo. And then you heard about me again, later that night in Harold's office. I was all Harold could talk about that day."

I tried to steal glances around the control room, hoping he would think it was only the look people have when they're searching for just the right words. I was searching for a lot more.

"It was quite a day for Harold," I said. "Getting reamed out by me and then seeing you and Dawn together. It must've surprised you when he told you about it. Some would think she'd be the logical one to blackmail, but Harold knew you were the one with more at stake. You didn't want her to have to choose between you and her money. That's why he figured you'd be better than she would. Let me see if I can guess how much he wanted…" I noticed the tape machine was running, though no sound was coming from the speakers. Robbie had set it to automatically rewind when it got to the end of the spot, then play it again.

"He wouldn't ask for too much at first. But, once you'd paid him it would just be the beginning. I'd say ten-thousand. Am I close?"

Winston laughed. "He actually said five. You've got more balls than he had, but it didn't matter. And it still doesn't," he added ominously.

"No, of course." What could I do? There were some empty metal tape reels hanging from a hook on the wall. If I got to them, could I throw them at him like frisbees? Pathetic.

"But before he sprang that on you," I continued, "while he was sampling the blow, he regaled you with the subject du jour, which was moi."

There was an electromagnet, used in bulk tape erasure, sitting on a shelf in the corner. Was it strong enough to attract a gun? Probably not, and even if it was, I'd have to plug it in first.

"He told you what a jerk I was that afternoon, what I'd said, how I'm a real hippie asshole, right? Probably waved my music in the air."

Winston was enjoying this. I guessed he had time before he had to be at the airport.

"Then he hit you with the bad news. I guess he didn't expect you to whip out a gun and shoot him; people never do. He sure looked surprised enough."

What the fuck could I possibly accomplish? We were in a recording studio, not an arsenal.

"Then you cleaned up the coke, except for leaving trace evidence on the desk, put my music in his hand, and swiped the Nixon picture."

There were some small demo reels stacked on the console. Even if I had time to grab one, so what? Could I try to strangle him with the tape? A bad feeling was creeping its way into my consciousness.

"You had to kill Dave Krulick," I went on, because what choice did I have? "He found out you were dealing coke to Harold, and that you were up there the night he was killed. And I think I can guess how he knew that."

I had him now, for whatever it was worth. He was hanging on my every word, an amused smirk on his face. The tape machine kept whirring, as it reached the end of the spot and then returned to the beginning to silently play again. Robbie had finished setting up the mix. He'd labeled the tracks on the board with a grease pencil, putting abbreviations above each fader, "LD VOC" for Eileen's lead vocal, "BKGD VOC" on several other tracks, the various instruments, and "VO" for Eileen's voice-over. The master faders were up but there was no sound because the individual tracks were down. But none of that was going to help me.

"Lick knew about it," I continued, "because they've got a new receptionist here, Tracy. This afternoon, when I was trying to make a call from her desk, I accidentally overheard George talking on another line. She said she'd been making that mistake all week."

Winston was nodding again, the smirk now a full-fledged grin. The gun never wavered from me as he casually leaned against Robbie's shoulder like they were two old pals, listening together. Robbie's terrified eyes stared at me.

"Lick must've been trying to make a call from her desk and overheard you talking on the phone to Harold." For the first time, the glimmering of an idea began to take shape. It was small and very desperate, but it was definitely a glimmering. "He probably heard you saying to Harold how good the 'product' was, or something like that, and that you'd be seeing him later that night." As I said this, I moved a little to my left, bringing me slightly closer to the console, which was just a foot or so away. I hoped it wouldn't register with him.

"When I saw Lick a couple of days later, and he'd found out I was one of the people who discovered the body, he was like a kid in a toy store. He spent a whole cab ride uptown making me tell him all the gruesome details." A little closer to the console. "That's how it seemed to him, like some kind of movie or TV show." A little more. "And then, when he remembered what he heard you say to Harold, he still didn't put it together. You couldn't be the one. Not his buddy, Todd, who was such a big fan."

Winston had stopped smiling. Now my back was to the console and, as I spoke, I leaned against it, hoping I was standing in the right place because I wouldn't be getting a chance to look back and make sure.

"You stopped by his apartment on Thursday night and, just like he wanted to hear all the stuff from me, he wanted to know from you if there was anything unusual going on at Harold's office. In his own, naive way, he probably hoped you'd seen the guy, and that the two of you could figure it out together."

I knew Eileen's voice-over began thirteen seconds into the spot. If Robbie had set the tape to play from the count-off, that would add another five seconds.

"You asked him if he'd told anyone else about it and, unfortunately for him, he hadn't. So you..."

Winston dropped the collegial pose with Robbie and stood straight up. "That's enough about Dave Krulick." I'd hit a nerve. It still bothered him that he had to kill Lick, and now I'd lost my rapport with the client.

"And that's enough about me," he said. "Let me tell you a little bit about you."

He stood behind Robbie and pointed the gun at me over the top of his head. The panic in Robbie's eyes intensified because he could no longer see Winston and didn't know what he was going to do. He needn't have worried because Winston wasn't paying attention to him.

"I'd heard about you long before George mentioned your fucking name," he told me. "You know, back in the '60s some of us cared more about serving our country than about saving our asses. And one of the people who cared was my older brother." The tape must be approaching the end of the spot by now, I thought.

"He volunteered for Vietnam. And he died there because people like you made our government too chickenshit to try and win the war. My brother died there because you, and others like you, sold him out. I'll never forget that." I heard a click as the tape began to rewind. "I used to hear your group on the radio back then, and I wanted to puke. *Body Bag Rag*." He spat out the words. "My brother came home in a fucking body bag, you filthy piece of shit."

The spot was now at the count-off. I'd once told Raymond I could write a 30-second jingle without a stopwatch, that's how good my sense of time had become. Now I was going to find out if it was true.

"I hadn't heard your name in years. But when George told me you'd be writing the Burger Meister spot, I thought, is he talking about the same Ernie Lanier, the fucking counterculture revolutionary? Is Ernie Lanier now writing jingles? For the corporate establishment he wanted to overthrow?" He laughed. "Well, it turned out you were, as Harold so nicely informed me." Five seconds gone by.

I tried to keep my face neutral as I slipped my hand behind me, searching for the fader. Instead, my fingers came in contact with something small, square, and flat. It was a cardboard sheath, containing a single-edged razor blade, the kind engineers use to splice tape and Brad Adonic had used to chop the cocaine lines. I tucked it into my palm, looking straight at Winston and trying to appear as engrossed as he'd been with me.

"Incidentally," he said, "I won't forget about your wife." Ten seconds gone by. "I'm not leaving forever. I'll be back in New York someday, and I intend to pay her a little visit. A nice, long, little visit." His voice dropped to a slimy whisper. "And I know she's going to show me a real—good—time."

I tried to maintain my expression, my insides curdling. Almost eighteen seconds. I slid the fader up, hoping it was the right one.

"Hey there, what are you doing?" Eileen's voice said.

For a split second, Winston thought it was coming from the darkened studio beyond the glass. He looked toward it, and in that instant I slammed Robbie's chair into him.

It caught him by surprise, knocking him backwards. His hand shot out, grabbing at the wires in the patch bay as he tried to stay on his feet. I saw no more than that, as I spun to my right, ducked around to the other side of the console and out the door to the studio.

HSST! *CRAACK*! Feedback and static exploded from the studio speakers. Winston must have partially pulled out some of the wires.

I realized there was no way I was going to make it to the exit. The rectangle of light that spilled into the studio from the control room covered the space I'd have to cross, and I didn't have time to sneak around it. Even if I could get that far, I'd be framed in the doorway. I desperately looked for a place to hide. In the drum booth? I'd be trapped like a rat in there. Behind one of the partitions? Too exposed. There was the piano, draped in its pads. I dove under it.

I heard his voice as he entered the studio.

"Hey asshole, what are you trying to prove? You're only making it worse on yourself."

I could sense him moving around. The loud crackling and hissing kept coming from the speakers, jabbing into my nervous system like a cattle prod. I had to ignore it. I had to think. Suddenly, the studio lights came on.

"There, that's better," he said.

Was this it? Was I going to wait here until he pulled up the padding and found me cowering underneath?

SIZZLE! *CRAACK*! It was like a storm, raging from the speakers.

"Now where would a draft dodger hide, besides Canada?" His voice sounded like he was over near the drum booth. "Nope, not in here." I heard his shoes slowly clacking their way across the hardwood floor and the sounds of partitions being moved around. His footsteps were getting closer. I slipped the razor blade out of its cardboard sheath.

"You're not getting out of this like you got out of the war, you fucking coward."

Now he was standing right next to the piano. I could see his patent leather loafers and the cuffs of his trousers, just beyond the edge of the padding.

"You're wasting your time, flower child. I'm gonna find you, and there's nothing you can do about it." His hand appeared at the bottom of the pad, as he began to lift it up. The razor blade was a heavy-duty one, and I hoped he was wearing nice, thin dress socks to go along with his snazzy shoes.

"Nope," he said, "not a single thing you can d…"

I grabbed his left leg and raked the blade across the back of his ankle as hard as I could. He let go of the padding and jumped back, pulling his leg from my grasp and cursing.

I turned and scuttled back under the piano as the shot tore through it, breaking a couple of strings and making them go *sploing*! in accompaniment to the sound of the gun, followed by a thud.

He must have lost his footing as he tried to crouch down and fire, and he'd fallen. The razor blade slipped out of my hand, but I didn't have time to look for it. I crawled out the other side, grabbing one of the pads and pulling it with me as I moved around the piano.

Winston was trying to get up, blood flowing from his ankle. If I hadn't severed his Achilles tendon completely, I'd at least slashed it pretty good. He was bringing the gun around and aiming it at me. I threw the padding over him just as he squeezed off a shot.

The bullet blew a hole in the padding, as tiny bits of stuffing flew out of it. He was knocked off balance again and went over, struggling to throw off the padding. I caught sight of a music stand nearby, grabbed the top of it and swung at him, catching him in the ribs with the heavy base of the stand as he emerged from under the padding and making him grunt. He still had the gun in his right hand.

I got in one more swing, but he saw it coming and tried to deflect it with his left forearm. It caught him flush on the elbow with a satisfyingly solid noise, making him clutch at it with his gun hand.

But my momentum had pulled me off kilter, and I stumbled, my back to him now as my foot caught on a microphone cable and I pitched forward onto the floor.

I rolled over, looked back toward him, and felt all hope drain out of me.

He was getting to his feet, still holding the gun, that fucking grin starting to come back to his face. His left arm hung by his side and his ankle was dripping blood onto the floor, but aside from that, he was right back in the saddle.

The speakers kept crackling. Maybe the reaction I'd always had to that sound was the premonition of my death, a feeling somehow that it would be the last sound I'd ever hear. And isn't dying the final act of helplessness?

Winston was standing now, regarding me.

"You're a real pain in the ass, you know? You deserve to die slowly, but lucky for you, I don't have the time."

I had no regrets, at least none I could think of in that moment. But with unbearable sadness, I thought of Annie, and that I'd never see her again. She wouldn't know until too late that a monster was coming for her. Could I warn her from the grave? Could I get in her dreams?

Winston took a step toward me and pulled the trigger. I saw his ankle give, simultaneous with the flash, as I dove to my right, scampering on my hands and knees behind the platform with the conductor's podium on it.

"Fuck," he muttered, as he moved to cut me off before I could come around the other end.

I came over the top instead, shoving the podium down onto him. He was almost able to elude it, but not quite. It clipped his injured elbow, and he shrieked in pain as I leaped off the platform and tackled him.

We landed on the floor in a tangled, struggling heap. I clawed at the gun, trying to wrench it from his hand. He heaved under me, flailing with his bad arm and trying to shake his gun hand out of my grip. All of a sudden, the gun was loose, skittering across the hardwood.

Now I was struggling to get off him, my eyes riveted on the gun, as he grabbed at my legs. I finally got free, only to slip on some of his blood and fall, sliding on my stomach and stopping just a few feet short of the gun. Winston tried to climb over me to get at it. I raised myself up under him, driving my head into his chest and knocking him off me, onto his bad arm. His howl of pain was topped by an especially loud *CRAACK*! from the speakers.

I crawled, in what seemed like agonizing slow motion, toward the gun, my hand straining forward, bare inches from it, my fingertips about to close around its handle as Winston landed heavily on top of me. The gun skittered even further away. The speakers were reaching a crescendo, as if they were ready to burst wide open.

The noise seemed to pour into me. I turned under him and reached up for his throat, wrapping my hands around it with strength I never knew I had, rising up and flipping us over.

I was on top of him now, squeezing the life out of him. He fought against me, but he had only one good arm, and it was as if my hands were welded to his windpipe. All I could see before me was a crimson fog through which his face appeared, bloated and grimacing, his eyes bugging out.

"NOTHING I CAN DO ABOUT IT?" I heard myself shouting over and over. Winston's eyes began to go glassy. He was gagging.

"Okay, okay, let's not kill him."

Raymond's voice pierced the fog. As if in a dream, I looked up from Winston and there he was, standing in the doorway, flanked by three uniformed cops, all with their guns drawn.

"Not bad for a peacenik," he said, giving it the once over. "You ever consider the military? You would've loved it in Nam."

Epilogue

"This is paradise?" I said, picking sand out of my teeth. "It's Coney Island with palm trees."

Annie and I were lying on the beach at Waikiki under a blazing sun and, just now, under the feet of a college kid going after a Frisbee.

"Sorry," he called out, leaping over us and making an acrobatic catch.

"College intersession," Annie sighed as she rolled onto her stomach, reached up behind her, and undid her top. "The first time we've ever stayed in a hotel together when we weren't either working or hiding, and it has to be college intersession." She picked up the suntan lotion and handed it over to me. "Here, do my back, would you?"

"If there weren't two-thousand people here," I said, "I would do your back, your front, and your bidding."

I spread the oil over her shoulder blades and moved my hands gently up and down her back, rubbing the sides of her breasts in passing.

"Mmmm, my bidding is opening up for bidness," she said. "But we can't just run back up to the room, can we? We only got down here five minutes ago."

I kissed the back of her neck, not minding the taste of the suntan lotion. "We're definitely staying on this beach. For all the money it costs and the week of work we're losing, we'd better stay on this beach."

She rolled onto her side and looked over at me, lightly clutching her bathing suit top against her and making me really want us to run back up to the room.

"I didn't marry Timothy Leary and I didn't marry Charles Bronson. I married Scrooge McDuck."

"Don't knock worrying about money. It sure beats worrying about health."

I lay back and squinted up at the sky. As I closed my eyes, the sun became a red haze with Winston's face in the middle of it. I remembered my hands, so loving a moment ago rubbing Annie's back, locked around his throat. I would've killed him, no doubt about it. I didn't like how that made me feel, and I hoped, someday, I would stop feeling it.

One of the few things Winston told the police was that Dawn had nothing to do with any of his crimes. He'd only used her as a source of information, encouraging her penchant for talking about herself, her activities, and the people she worked with.

For her part, she must've thought it was wonderful to be with someone who, unlike Gerard, was so interested in her career.

"What a comedy of errors that was with Dawn," Annie said, as if in synch with my thoughts.

Two weeks had gone by, and it was never far from mind. We'd say things like that to each other, out of context, remembering little pieces of it.

When Dawn finally called back, Annie told her she knew her boyfriend was Fred and tried to warn her. Dawn thought she'd lost her mind, which lead to several minutes of frantic miscommunication, finally straightened out.

"When she told me his name," Annie said now, "and I knew you were at Magnum Opus, I almost died."

"You and me both, kid."

She raised herself off the towel, I took her in my arms, and we kissed. I didn't care if half the undergraduate population of America was watching.

She sighed contentedly and settled back down on her stomach.

When she'd called Raymond, she was practically screaming Winston's name into the phone at him, while he was saying it to her at the same time.

That's because he'd just found out who registered Boom Box and Spar. Winston had conveniently done both under his present name, which wasn't, of course, his real name. In Chicago his fingerprints matched someone they were looking for named Jonathan Kent. In L.A. he'd apparently been Peter Benson, and the name on his new phony driver's license was Richard Hedges. Maybe his goal was to become the Marlboro man.

There was no evidence that George Magnus knew anything about what was going on. When the police searched Winston's warehouse they found, in addition to my bass and some drug paraphernalia, a half-constructed recording studio. He'd been planning, with the help of Dawn's money, to steal the clients he'd gotten at Magnum Opus, add them to his agency customers, and start his own jingle house and cocaine concession. He probably would've done very well.

I closed my eyes again, and the sun was no longer Winston's face. The sound of the ocean and the babble of voices around us melted into a dreamy soup. Somewhere nearby a radio was playing. I was just dozing off when something bounced against my head.

"Sorry!" yelled a young male voice as I sat up with a jolt.

A skinny kid with long hair and acne was scooping up a volleyball next to our towels. "My girlfriend hit it," he said apologetically. "She really sucks at volleyball." He ran off to rejoin the game, spraying sand behind him.

We lay back down, I took Annie's hand, and we both drifted into a pleasant, if cacophonous, reverie. Another radio was now playing, in competition with the first one. David Bowie and Bruce Springsteen were battling it out, but as long as neither of them turned to static, I thought I could take it.

The song to our left finished and Bowie's voice was replaced by Brad Adonic. He was singing the new Burger Meister jingle.

We're Burger Meister People
Our burgers are our pride
We pat 'em down, and flip 'em round
And spread those buns real wide
We're Burger Meister People
We're always number one
And even if you like them rare
You know they'll be well done

"I think I hear Dawn in the backup group," said Annie.

"I wouldn't be surprised. This, incidentally, was why Hook and DiMango were acting so funny towards me. I thought it had something to do with Gordell, but it was actually because they were going after Burger Meister and didn't want me to find out."

"Wonderful business, isn't it?"

"Don't know where we'd be without it."

A drop of water plopped down against my nose, and I opened my eyes to see that the sky had turned cloudy and it was starting to rain. After a second or two, it really began pouring in earnest. All around us, people were hurriedly gathering up blankets, towels, coolers, radios and surf boards, and getting out of there.

Annie fastened her bathing suit top and picked up her towel. "Race you back to the room?"

"I've got a better idea," I said, watching the exodus. "Have you ever made love on a deserted, rainy beach?"

She looked around, checking out the situation. "But they can see us from the hotel."

"Not if we're behind this tree," I said, leading her over to a wide and leafy palm.

She gave me a secretive smile and started to undo her top again. Her body glistened with rain and suntan oil and her hair was sopping wet.

"What if it's a jingle rain?" she said. "Sixty seconds and it's over?"

"We'll just have to leave that up to the Ultimate Client," I said, cupping her face in my hands and kissing her softly.

It rained and rained like it would never stop.

Also by this author

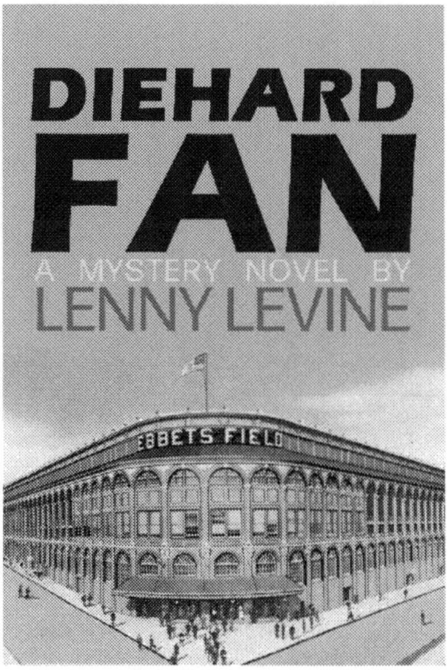

Eddie Fein is a twelve-year-old boy living in Brooklyn. It's the last week of the 1951 baseball season, and his beloved Dodgers are enduring the epic collapse to the hated Giants that will be punctuated by Bobby Thomson's "shot heard 'round the world."

Eddie's love for the Dodgers springs from his love for his father Barry Fein, a passionate Dodger fan, but an alcoholic who's prone to bouts of depression and anger.

When two Giant fans are murdered, Nick DiFazio, lead detective on the case and Barry's best friend, is afraid of what his suspicions are telling him.

Eddie somehow learns of Nick's feelings. He secretly embarks on a desperate mission to prove his father's innocence, a quest that only seems to worsen things.

In the meantime, and throughout, we witness the Dodgers' final week, sometimes through radio and TV, sometimes from the playing field itself.

And as Bobby Thomson crushes Ralph Branca's fastball into baseball history, Eddie will learn the terrifying truth.